REUNION

A TEMPERANCE FALLS ROMANCE

LONDON HALE

Reunion

LONDON HALE

Edited by Lisa Hollett of Silently Correcting Your Grammar, LLC

Cover Art © Brighton Walsh

Digital ISBN: 978-1-944336-37-0

Paperback ISBN: 978-1-944336-38-7

For inquiries, contact London Hale at london@londonhale.com

LONDON HALE

Dedicated to all thouse who skipped their high school reunions to avoid awkward situations.

Luke wouldn't have been there anyway.

chapter one

LUKE

WHOEVER SAID YOU could never go back home again was definitely on to something. Even though I still lived in Temperance Falls, it wasn't the place that felt off now, but the *people*.

I sat at a dining table, staring at two guys I'd once considered my best friends. Forcing myself to smile. Forcing myself to participate in the conversation. Talking to people I didn't have anything in common with was something I did every night at Pops' Hops—my brewery, my baby. This should've been no different.

Except I *had* had something in common with these people at one point—ten long years ago, when we'd been in high school. Back then, we'd been the best of friends. Hell, one of them was *family*. A family he no longer cared to be part of, but family nonetheless.

Barry, my stepbrother, had bailed after his father had passed away. Graduated then fled and never looked back, despite the fact that my mom had cared for him when he had no one left. Despite the fact that his father—a family man and the only person I'd ever called Dad—would hate Barry running out on the people my stepfather had loved with all his heart.

But Barry was an asshole. There was no getting around it. He was the kind of guy I kicked out of the brewery for getting handsy with the female bartenders. The kind of guy who belittled others to make himself feel better. The kind of guy his dad would've been ashamed he'd turned into. Even under those circumstances, I still thought of him as family.

And that made me the most loyal dumbass in the world.

"Seriously, you should've seen the tits on this one!" Barry said, gesturing in front of his chest as if his words weren't enough to get his point across. Never mind the fact that it wasn't just a bunch of guys shooting the shit. Aaron and his wife, Jessica, sat across the table from me. She slid a look to Aaron, making her displeasure over his friends known. That'd teach him for offering up his summer home as the location for our pre-reunion barbecue tonight. Good intentions and all that, but it'd been raining too hard to do any sort of grilling. Which meant we were all stuck inside, in close quarters, with nothing much to do as we waited for one other person to join us...the only person who'd make this bearable for me.

Hannah.

The girl I'd lusted after in high school—hell, the woman who still visited me in my fantasies—and one of my best friends, despite our not having seen each other in ten years.

Barry, never knowing when to stop, continued. "More than a mouthful, if you know what I mean. Damn, haven't seen a set that nice in a while. Fucking Hannah cockblocked me, though. And I think everyone here knows she doesn't have anything in the titty department to write home about."

Just hearing her name from his lips had my jaw clenching, my eyes focused on the bottle of beer I twisted in my hand, never mind the derogatory words he spewed. Even my best brew couldn't salvage tonight. Barry's callous disregard for Hannah grated on my nerves—*had* grated on my nerves since day fucking one—and made me even more frustrated that she was still with him. Or at least sort of. On-again, off-again—just like they'd been since high school. Since I'd confided in my brother that I liked a girl and wanted to ask her out. Since he'd beat me to the punch and stole her right out from under me.

Yeah, I was still bitter. Anyone would be, especially when it was someone like Hannah on the line. She was *gorgeous*, but it wasn't just her looks. She was sweet and caring, compassionate and gentle— basically, the opposite of Barry. I had no idea what she saw in him.

Hannah and I were long-distance friends, something I blamed Barry for. He'd always been jealous of our relationship and had done everything he could to keep us apart. So we'd text and e-mail, reply to each other on social media. We even had an occasional phone call. It was never enough, but what choice did I have? Steal my stepbrother's girlfriend? That'd make me no better than him.

"What about you, man?" Barry clapped a hand on my shoulder, pulling me out of my thoughts. "It's been too long. I miss swapping stories." By stories, he meant tales of his sexual prowess, and by swapping, he meant forcing me to listen to the different ways he got his dick wet all the while keeping Hannah on a leash. All the while knowing how I felt about her.

Yup. Asshole.

I shrugged. "Not many stories to swap. I keep pretty busy at the brewery."

"A brewery, huh? Gotta hand it to you—I thought my dad's hobby was lame as hell, but you went and turned it into a real business. Bet it gets you lots of pussy, doesn't it?"

Jessica shoved her chair back and shot her husband a look. "I think I'll go call Hannah and make sure she can find the house okay in all the rain."

"Hey, will you tell her to pick me up a couple bottles of Malbec?" Barry yelled to Jessica's retreating form. "Beer's not really my thing." He glanced at me and gestured to his mostly full bottle of the specialty brew I'd brought. The specialty brew I'd made. One of his dad's recipes, actually, but I didn't tell him that. "And, hey," he called toward the doorway Jessica had disappeared through, "can you bring in some snacks or something? I'm fucking starving."

"She's not a servant, man," Aaron said, his tone sharp. "There's a full spread in the kitchen. Help yourself."

Barry laughed, then saluted like a jackass. "Got it. No orders to her unless it's in the bedroom. You can tell me all about that later." He pushed back from the table and headed into the kitchen, smiling the whole way.

"Shit, when did he turn into such an asshole?" Aaron asked under his breath before he cringed. "Sorry."

"For what? He *is* an asshole."

Aaron chuckled then lifted his chin toward where Barry had disappeared. "Brothers and all."

Brothers in name only. I shrugged, not wanting to get into it. Barry was staying here for the weekend because of the reunion festivities, not going back to the mainland until Sunday. And even though I had a nice little house I could flee to, we'd be around each other a lot more than we had been in ten long years. I didn't want to open up a can of worms to deal with.

"Believe me, no offense taken," I said, waving him off.

He smiled and tipped his beer bottle toward me. "Just be glad you can escape. I'm stuck with him all weekend. No fucking idea why I thought it'd be a good plan to offer up my house."

"I'll leave extra beer."

He laughed just as the doorbell rang, and Jessica rushed past to open the front door. The porch light shone outside, illuminating the rain coming down in heavy sheets, bolts of lightning going off simultaneously with the nearly constant rumbles of thunder. But none of that held my attention like the woman standing in the doorway did.

"You must be Hannah," Jessica said. "Come in, come in." She shut the door behind Hannah then took her bag from her, setting it down on the rug while Hannah shivered in the entryway.

Even soaked to the bone, she was the most gorgeous woman I'd ever laid eyes on. I hadn't seen her in the flesh in way too long, and the pictures on her social media didn't do her justice. Her dark hair was pulled back in a ponytail, the rain causing some strands to stick to her face. Her eyes looked black from here, but I knew they were green on the outside with a burst of brown around her pupil. She was still as petite as ever—I had at least a foot and probably close to a hundred pounds on her—but her soft curves managed to make my mouth water and my cock harden, just like always. That reaction didn't lessen as I took in her flushed cheeks and full, pink lips. Combined with the damp hair at her temples, she looked freshly fucked.

And goddamn if I didn't want to see that look on her face while she was in my bed.

"Hannah, hey!" Aaron said, getting up to give her a quick hug. "Haven't seen you in years. How've you been?"

"I'm good, thanks. You seem to be doing well if you're living on this side of the island. That's wonderful, Aaron. And thank you so much for having us all over." She smiled at Aaron and Jessica, never once looking in my direction. "Though I hope no one has anywhere to be tonight. I don't think the bridge is going to be passable."

Before I could contemplate what that meant, Barry came strolling in from the kitchen. "Banana! 'Bout time you got here. My bed's not gonna warm itself." He reached for her, tugging her into his side as I curled my hands into fists, my jaw clenching. The cringe I swore I saw sweep across her face had to be a trick of the light. "And no bridge, huh? You hear that, Luke? Looks like you're stuck here for the night."

"Luke?" She snapped her head up, looking around until her eyes landed on me. The biggest grin spread across her face, and it was a sucker punch to the stomach. Jesus, I felt like I was seventeen all over again when she looked at me like that.

She slipped out from under Barry's arm and walked straight for me, her smile never faltering. I didn't even have time to stand before she had me enveloped in a hug, tucking herself right in between my spread legs, her arms tight around my neck, my face too close to her tits for what was acceptable friend behavior. "Hey, stranger."

Jesus, that voice in my ear would be my undoing. The breathy whisper, the brush of her lips against my skin… Two little words that didn't mean anything, but combined with the feel of her in my arms and her light, citrusy scent surrounding me, it was a memory I'd definitely stroke myself off to later.

I brought my arms around her, hugging her as

close as I dared. I wanted to say a hundred things to her, most of them questioning her sanity at still being involved with my asshole brother. But all that came out was, "Hey, Hannah."

"All right, you two, break it up." Barry laughed as he tugged Hannah away, but I could hear the strain in his voice. Hannah's and my friendship had always been a thorn in his side. Probably because he knew exactly how I felt about her.

"You're staying here, too?" she asked me, her eyes hopeful.

I shook my head. "Hadn't planned on it. You sure the bridge is out?"

"Definitely. I almost didn't make it across. The water's completely over the road."

"Well, shit."

Aaron's home sat on a tiny island off the western side of Temperance Falls, a short bridge connecting the two. A bridge that was my only way to the main island and was also prone to flooding. Tomorrow was Friday, one of the busiest days at the brewery. I had shit that needed to be done, and I didn't want to leave my partner, AJ, in the lurch. But it didn't look like I had much of a choice.

"You can stay here," Aaron said. "There's a pullout couch in the basement."

"The basement?" Barry said. "What's he need to go to the basement for? There's an empty room right next to mine. Hannah wouldn't mind giving up the room for you, Luke. Besides, we all know she'll end up in my bed anyway. Isn't that right, Banana?" He tugged her to him, and that time I knew it wasn't a trick of the light when she cringed and pulled away, her words only confirming my thoughts.

"Barry, stop."

"What? It's the truth. Come on, you don't wanna send Luke down there when there's a perfectly good bed upstairs, now do you?"

Oh, fuck no. He wasn't going to manipulate her into agreeing to something on my behalf. "The basement's fine with me," I cut in before Hannah could say anything. "Thanks, Aaron."

"No, Luke, it's okay." She sighed, a heavy sound, and waved me off. The girl with the vibrant smile was gone, and in her place was someone just getting by. "Please. Take the room. I'm fine with Barry."

"Knew you'd see it my way." Barry reached down to slap her ass. "Now who's up for a game of poker?"

Hannah shook her head, already heading toward her bag by the front door. "I'm out. I had to be at work by four this morning, and I'm wiped. I don't want to be rude, but I really need to get some sleep so I can function tomorrow."

"Aw, Banana, if you wanted to get into my bed faster, why didn't you say so?" Barry sauntered over to her, tossing us a wave as he headed upstairs in front of Hannah, leaving her to carry her bag herself.

With a sigh and an eye roll, she gathered her things and followed Barry. I really hoped what she said was true—that she was just exhausted and this wasn't who she'd become. She looked so goddamn weary as she trudged up the steps. At least until she looked my way, catching my eye. And then she smiled. Just a tip of her lips, but it was enough for me.

It had to be.

"You going to head up, too?" Aaron asked.

It was barely ten o'clock and way too early for my usual bedtime. Since opening the brewery, I usually stayed up until two, sometimes three in the morning. But Aaron and Jessica looked hopeful, so I nodded. "You don't happen to have an extra toothbrush, do you?"

"Yeah, I think so. Come on up, and I'll grab you some clothes, too."

Once in my room, I grabbed my phone to shoot a quick text to my partner. *Bridge is flooded. I'm stuck here for the night. Not sure when I'll be able to get in. I'll keep you posted.*

AJ's reply came almost instantaneously. *Stuck with Hannah and Barry together? Perfection.*

I could read the sarcasm in his reply, so I sent him the middle finger emoji.

Seconds later, another message popped up. *And don't worry about Hops. I've got it handled however long you need.*

One less thing weighing down my mind, I settled on the bed in my borrowed sweats. As soon as we'd come up here, Aaron and Jessica had immediately escaped to the solitude of their room at the end of the hall. I envied them that. The two extra bedrooms were clustered together, the walls thin enough that I could hear bits of conversation from the other side. And, of course, the bed had to be against the shared wall.

I almost got up half a dozen times and went to the basement and the pullout couch just to avoid hearing this. But doing that was like spitting in the face of Hannah's offering. The thing that kept tripping me up was why she was supposed to stay in this room anyway. Last I heard—from her, no less—she and Barry were on-again. And if she were on with *me*, there was no fucking way she'd be spending the night anywhere but in my bed.

Except she wasn't in my bed. She was in Barry's.

As if to punctuate my thoughts, a groan echoed from next door, the sound distinct through the walls. Jesus Christ, if I had to sit there and listen to them fuck, I'd swim the goddamn lake and walk home just to avoid it.

But instead of moaning, Barry's booming voice came through the wall, the volume high enough that I heard it clearly. "Quit being so difficult." Then just the cadence of words, not spoken loud enough that I could make them out. As desperately as I didn't want to hear any of it, I also had a sick fascination with what Hannah's response might be. I hoped she was shoving him off her, making him sleep on top of the covers instead of under them. Or, hell, sending his ass to the basement.

The curiosity got to me, and I leaned closer to the wall, hoping she'd make my night and tell him to fuck off. Instead, her voice rang out, clear and firm enough for me to catch every word. "You haven't made me come in six years, Barry. Why would tonight be any different?"

I froze, uncertain I'd heard her correctly, but from the raised tone of Barry's voice a second later, there was no more doubt. He was pissed, shouting the kinds of bullshit a wounded ego brought about. Holy shit. Barry, the asshole who bragged about every conquest he had, who went on and on about how he'd made Hannah scream time and again, hadn't been able to make her come? For six fucking *years*?

I'd always taken her at her word that she was happy—no, that wasn't true. She'd never said she was *happy*. She was always fine, and I'd accepted that. But being in her presence, seeing her in person for the first time in so long, feeling her body up against mine… How could I ignore it? Especially when I knew she wasn't happy. Especially when I knew she wasn't even *satisfied*.

I clenched my teeth, trying to remind myself this was my brother's girlfriend. Yes, he was an asshole, but was that enough to make me cross a line I had no business crossing? For ten years since he'd walked out the door without a backward glance, I'd held on to the idea that we were brothers, even when he could barely return a phone call. When he couldn't even speak to my mother on her birthday or Mother's Day. When he couldn't be bothered to be a decent human being.

He didn't deserve Hannah. And she sure as hell didn't deserve to be treated like that. She deserved a guy who sent her flowers just because, who called her out of the blue to tell her he loved her. At the very least, she deserved a guy who could make her come.

And I was definitely up for the challenge.

chapter two

HANNAH

WHAT HAD I gotten myself into? For twelve years—almost half of my life—I'd been putting up with Barry's shit. Oh sure, it'd all started out normal. He was sweet in high school, kind even. Attentive. We had chemistry then. But a few years later when we headed off to college together, things had started to change. It'd been subtle at first, almost unnoticeable. His words had grown a little less loving, his actions a little less attentive. We'd been together for seven years before I really noticed the switch—I'd assumed we'd cooled off into a standard, albeit stale, relationship. We had passed college and moved out into the world to start our jobs and our lives, to move forward together when I started to wonder if I was making a mistake.

And then two years ago, I'd found out about the other woman.

Women, really.

By then the job I chose, the one I loved, had beaten me down to the point that I simply didn't care as much about life outside the hospital as I probably should have. Being a nurse in a busy emergency room was no joke, and it took all my attention and energy. I needed a support system, something I didn't have living with Barry in the city. I only had him, so I dealt with his shit. Oh sure, I broke up with him and moved out after I knew about the first affair, but I always let him back when he came begging. I always forgave his mistakes. I bought the "never again" bullshit he served me, even while keeping him slightly at arm's length. Until the last time six months ago. That one had hurt—she'd been someone I knew. Someone I trusted. That one, I doubted we would ever come back from.

But being back on Temperance Falls, seeing people I had always thought of as true friends, had left me feeling off-kilter. I hadn't realized how much I'd missed being home until I'd driven over the bridge to the island I grew up on. That homesickness brought with it a nostalgic sense of something tied up completely in Barry and our memories together.

This weekend was going to be an emotional roller coaster.

"I had no intention of sleeping in the same room with you," I said as I pushed past him into the little guest bedroom. One bed sat in the middle with a chair by the window. Those were my options. Barry or a backache from the chair. Thank God I brought my yoga mat.

Barry shut the door behind him and huffed as if laughing at me. Dismissing my irritation as usual. "I'm doing you a favor, Banana. You can't be in a room with anyone else—you snore."

Wait…I…did I? No. No way. Someone would have told me. Someone other than Barry. But there had never been someone other than Barry, and I hadn't slept in the same room with anyone else since high school sleepovers with my friends. What if… "I do not snore."

"Yeah, you do, but it's cute, so I deal. Now come here, little girl. I haven't seen you in weeks."

Of course he hadn't—I was good at avoiding him until my emotions got too raw from watching people die. Eventually, he'd corner me and drag me off to have martinis or specialty cocktails I couldn't pronounce, wouldn't want to drink, and couldn't pay for on my salary.

"Look, Barry. This…us…it's not happening again. We're done for good this time."

"Sure we are." He smirked as he tugged off his shirt, leering my way when his hands dropped to the buckle on his belt. "You say that, but you don't mean it."

I groaned loud and long, so damn tired of him. "I do mean it."

He lunged, grabbing me right off the ground and pinning my arms to the sides as he tried to kiss me. That bastard. I jerked and pulled away, hating when he picked me up. Hating to be overpowered by him. He knew that, knew I hated the nickname they'd all called me in elementary school, too. He simply didn't care. About me, about my opinions, about anything other than himself.

"Stop, Barry."

"Quit being so difficult," he snapped. He dropped me onto the bed and pushed his pants over his hips, keeping one hand on my hip to hold me in place as he brought out his saccharine-sweet voice. "C'mon, baby. You know we're good together. Let me remind you." He crawled closer, making the tightness in my chest grow. The fury in my gut burn hotter. "Let me between those stubby little legs so I can make you come."

Oh, fuck no. My anger made my voice a little sharper than I'd intended, a little louder, too. "You haven't made me come in six years, Barry. Why would tonight be any different?"

His face went blank, his eyes practically emptying of life as I watched. *Shit.*

"You're a real bitch, you know that?" He jumped up from the bed, snatching his shirt from the floor and yanking it over his head. "You used to come home stinking of vomit and shit and that preservative stuff from the labs, and I was expected to just accept it. To pretend you're sexy when you look like death and smell like it, too. Maybe if you hadn't worked so much, you would have been easier to deal with. Or hey, how about you not cry all the time? Then maybe you'd be a little more responsive. It's not my fault you're fucking frigid." He stormed into the bathroom and slammed the door behind him.

That…went just as I'd figured. God, he always turned things around to be my fault. Why had I never noticed that?

Hell, if I was honest, I had noticed. I'd just been too stupid to care. Or too tired. Or too…me.

Not wanting to sit around and wait for more from him, I slipped out the bedroom door and headed downstairs. I needed air and space, needed time to think. I needed a new life, a change of pace or scenery. Something different from what I'd been putting up with for so many years. I needed…a beer.

My pace quickened, my feet turning the wrong direction a time or two while taking me to the kitchen. I so rarely drank—something that annoyed Barry to no end. I worked so much and was on call so often that it was always bad timing for me to get tipsy. But tonight was different. I was off for four whole days and on the island again for our high school reunion. The storm meant we wouldn't be going anywhere, which meant I could drink and relax and hunker down in the beautiful house of our friend Aaron. A beer sounded perfect.

The refrigerator was packed with food, but on the bottom shelf sat rows upon rows of brown bottles with red labels. A Pops' Hops logo beckoned, and I grinned as I reached for one. Luke's beer—from *his* brewery. I had wanted so badly to come back when he'd opened the place, but Barry claimed he'd had to work, and I hadn't owned a car then, so I'd been stuck. I'd also bought a car two months later because I had been tired of being reliant on Barry while we were still living together. He'd laughed at it—said my little beater wouldn't last a year. She'd been with me for almost two years and had gotten me back home through the massive storms sweeping the Midwest. We showed him.

God, I needed to stop thinking about my ex.

I yanked off the bottle cap with the opener on the counter and took a deep pull from the beer. Cold, crisp, mellow. So good. Perfect for a summer night in the middle of a storm. Luke had such a talent, such a skill. And with that killer smile and those blue eyes, the muscled body that screamed sexual prowess…he had to be the most eligible bachelor on the island. No wonder Barry never came back—he couldn't compete with his own stepbrother.

"I really need to learn to stop being so petty," I said to myself before taking another drink.

"Usually, when people start talking to themselves, I cut them off."

I choked, coughing hard as my eyes found…holy hell. "Shit, Luke. I didn't hear you come in."

"Sorry, I didn't mean to scare you." He stepped closer, the muscles of his abs clenching with every move. Muscles, as in multiple. And abs, as in bare. The man was shirtless and…much more decorated than I remembered him being. "Is there room for one more?"

"Yeah, sure." I nodded, trying hard to tear my eyes from the lines and swirls covering portions of his arms and chest. Good God, the man was a work of art in more ways than one. As if those bright eyes and panty-melting smile weren't enough, he was also gorgeous. Tall and muscular and tattooed in a way that accented every dip. He was positively lickable. And I was staring. "Would you like a beer?"

He held my gaze, not looking away for a moment. "I think I could use about twenty."

I blinked, something dark and warm swirling deep in my belly. Something like appreciation. Like arousal. Something I should not have been feeling for my boyfriend's brother.

Okay, ex-boyfriend's stepbrother.

God, the details didn't make it any better.

Yeah, really needed to stop staring. "Right. Beer." I took a step toward the refrigerator, but Luke was faster. So much more…aggressive.

"Sit down. You don't need to wait on me." He turned, showing me the full palette of his back. The shades of black and gray, the muscles.

I needed to sit down, all right. I edged onto a stool at the kitchen island, watching as he grabbed a beer from the refrigerator and opened it. Nearly shaking as he stalked closer and took the seat next to mine. So close.

Too close.

"I like this," I said, indicating the bottle so he knew what I was talking about. "I really do. Everything about it tastes like summer."

The smile he shot me was more humble than usual but no less devastating. "Thanks. It's our latest. Haven't even debuted it at Hops yet. AJ calls it summer in a bottle."

"He's right—that's exactly what it made me think

of." I took another sip before setting the bottle against my thigh. "I've been wanting to get back so I can see the place. I hope to find time this weekend." I shook my head, my lips twisting into a frown. "I should've come when you opened."

"Nah, don't worry about it. You've been busy being a lifesaving rock star."

"Rock star might be selling it a little much. Pretty sure rock stars don't come home with blood on their shoes."

"I think rock star might not be enough. Seriously, Hannah, what you do—" He shook his head, staring at the beer in his hand before catching my eye again. "It takes a lot of heart. Though, that's something you've always had in spades."

I looked down, biting back my smile. A man gave me a compliment, and I practically turned into a blushing schoolgirl. What was wrong with me? "Thanks. It's hard, but I love it. I really do." I picked at the edge of the label on my bottle, the warmth of the buzz from the beer making my mouth a little looser than usual. "Other people, not so much."

His lips turned down, his eyes narrowing in a way that made me think I'd somehow pissed him off. "Other people are assholes."

Ah, not me. Barry. "Yeah, well…some things don't change." I took one more drink, loving the way the beer made my brain a little fuzzy. "What about you? I mean, other than the fact that you're probably not an asshole, what is it I don't know about you? What haven't you shared with me yet?"

"Wow, you're starting off with the hard-hitting questions, huh? No small talk."

"What was it your mom used to say? Small talk is for small minds."

His brows lifted, and he sat back a little. Luke had obviously forgotten how much time I'd spent at their house back in school. "She still says it. Doesn't have time for that bullshit," he said with a laugh. "Okay, something I haven't told you yet." He bit his lip, an act I felt all the way between my legs. "You sure you want to hear this?"

I couldn't look away from his mouth. "Give it to me."

"Do you want serious or stupid? Because I've got both."

"Ooh, options." I tapped my chin, looking up to the ceiling as if giving his question considerable thought. "Serious. I'm good with serious."

Luke shook his head and rolled his eyes a little, still smiling. Still too fucking hot for his own good. "Serious truth I don't share... I'm terrified the brewery's going to fail and I'll have nothing left. No job. No money. End up having to live with my mom again."

"Wow." I sat back, draining the last of my beer. "That really is serious."

"You should've picked stupid. Though I'm sort of glad you didn't. It's embarrassing as hell." He winked. The man fucking winked. I might as well have died right there in the kitchen.

"I'm totally going to want to hear that one,

but first…" I leaned forward and put my hand on his, making sure I had his full attention. "You're charming, smart, and completely committed to your business. I see it online, I hear it from people who still live here. You could never fail so long as you keep trying the way you do." I tapped his hand and sat back, grinning. "But also, your mom makes excellent chocolate chip cookies. Living with her might not be as bad as you think."

Luke laughed quietly, his shoulders shaking. "That she does. And thank you. Seriously, hearing that from you means a lot." He held my gaze, smiling softly. Looking at me as if he wanted…something I couldn't even fathom. "Now your turn."

This could be dangerous. I hopped up and grabbed two more beers from the refrigerator, pulling off the caps before reclaiming my seat next to Luke. And if that seat happened to inch a little closer to him? All the better. "Serious or stupid?"

"I can't have both?"

I pursed my lips in a fake scowl. "You're greedy."

"When it comes to you? Always."

Wait…was he flirting with me? And was I… liking it?

Yes. Totally yes. So I took a deep breath, and I said the one thing I really shouldn't have. "I think your brother is an asshole."

Luke choked on his beer, his eyes going large for a moment before he recovered. "Everyone thinks my brother's an asshole. I just assumed you didn't see it. Or chose not to."

I focused on the bottle in my hand, picking at the edges of the label. Not willing to look into his eyes. "I'm really good at schedules, you know? Order. This, then this, then that, then the next. Routines are what save my sanity. Accepting his assholeness became just another habit almost. I'm not really sure how that happened, though." I shook my head, tearing the label off in one piece. Success.

"That's supposedly a sign of sexual frustration, you know." He nodded toward the bottle when I jerked my head up.

"Really?" I took a drink as he nodded. Funny, I'd been peeling labels for years. "Fitting."

Luke went silent, but he didn't need to say anything to hold my attention. Something in his eyes, in the way he looked into mine, captivated me. He didn't talk, didn't move, didn't do anything but watch me for a few long moments. Long enough that I started to get nervous when he finally leaned closer.

"So is it true then?"

"Is what true?"

"Our rooms share a wall. I heard the…fight."

My brain tried to rewind the evening, but I was a little too tipsy. I remembered being upstairs, talking to Barry. But a fight? "I'm not following you."

"Has it really been six years?"

Something stuttered to life in my memory. Something about sex. With Barry. Something I'd said about it being six years since… "Oh God, you heard that?"

I jumped up, my face blazing hot. He'd heard *that*.

Of all the things, of all the complaints Barry could have said that Luke would have known about me, he had to hear *that* one. That I was broken, prudish. Frigid.

Luke grabbed my hand, tugging me into his space. My hips brushed his knees as he dragged me between his spread thighs until I was right up against him. Touching him. Craving him. He didn't stop there, though. Oh, no. He looked right into my eyes as he raised a hand and brushed my hair behind my ear. So gentle. So affectionate.

If the growing wetness of my panties was any indication, I wasn't as broken as Barry had made me believe.

"When's the last time someone made you scream, Hannah?"

Definitely not broken. "I—"

Before I could say more, the sound of footsteps on the stairs made me jump back. Aaron appeared in the kitchen, sliding to a stop when he noticed the two of us. "Oh, hey. Sorry to interrupt—"

"You're not interrupting anything," I said, my voice a little too high. My words spoken a little too fast. I was a horrible liar.

Luke shot me another wink before turning to look toward Aaron. "What's up, man?"

"I just came down to make sure the sump pump was working. I don't want to wake up to a new lake in my basement."

"Need some help?"

Aaron headed for the basement stairs across the kitchen. "Nope, but thanks. I think I've got this."

He disappeared through the doorway, leaving Luke and me alone once more. I clung to my beer bottle, my back against the cabinets across from the island. Needing space.

Luke didn't seem to want to give it.

He stepped closer, slipping through the shadowy room with ease. Silent. Stealthy. So fucking sexy.

"Longer than six years, I assume?"

Oh God, back to that. Something in the way he said the words, the way he watched me so intently, gave me a courage I'd never felt before. Loosened my lips even more than the beer could have.

"Never," I said, trying hard not to notice the way his jaw ticked. How his stare grew more intense. "No one's ever—"

"Hey, Luke," Aaron yelled from downstairs. "I think I'm going to need a hand, after all."

Luke didn't miss a beat. "Yeah, I'll be right there." He kept his eyes on mine as he leaned closer, running his thumb over my bottom lip and making me go weak in the knees. "Just so you know, I'm up for the challenge."

I closed my eyes and fell back against the counter, not breathing until I heard his footsteps head down the stairs. Did he just…? No. He didn't. He wouldn't have. Luke wasn't the type of guy to make a move like that. He'd never looked at me as more than a friend, or even worse, as Barry's girl.

Yet my lips still tingled from where he'd touched me, and my panties were still wet from whatever had just happened between us. Something had changed, and I wasn't sure if I should like it or be afraid.

Maybe a little of both.

With weak knees and a racing heart, I hurried up the stairs and slipped back into the room I was to share with Barry. I didn't look at Luke's door at all as I passed, too worried I'd head that way instead if I even glanced at it. Barry was asleep when I entered, which was at least a small blessing. I definitely didn't want to have to explain where I'd been.

I grabbed a pillow and a blanket off the bed and curled up in the chair, staring at the wall that separated this from Luke's room. Wondering when he'd come back upstairs. Wondering if he'd be thinking about me over there. If he'd end up as turned on by our kitchen encounter as I was. Would he…take care of things? Stroke himself while thinking of me? Would he groan loud enough for me to hear it, knowing I'd be listening?

Would I be able to resist him if he did?

chapter three

AFTER HELPING AARON in the basement for more than an hour last night, I'd had some misguided fantasies of Hannah waiting for me in my bedroom. They'd varied, everything from her pacing the room while muttering to herself, totally lost in thought, to her reading a book in the side chair, to her gloriously naked and sprawled out in my bed. Sadly, the bed—and the room—had been empty, and since Aaron and I had been in the basement where the previously offered pullout couch sat, that only meant one thing.

She'd gone back into Barry's room.

The thought had driven me crazy all fucking night, making me toss and turn as I'd wondered about the possibilities. Had she gotten in bed with him? Slipped right under the covers and pressed her body against his? Had I gotten her so worked up she'd decided to see if he could actually do his job and make his girl come?

And there'd been no mistaking it—Hannah had been aroused last night while we'd been in the kitchen together. Horny as hell if my radar was spot-on, and it usually was.

But had it been circumstance? Or *me*?

Rain still battered the windows, the guest room dark even though it was eight in the morning. The storm had continued all through the night and showed no signs of quitting, which meant I was stuck here, at least until the bridge cleared of water. Though stuck here certainly had a whole new meaning after the interaction last night with Hannah.

After a quick shower in the en suite bathroom, I put on my day-old jeans—commando because I wasn't recycling my boxer briefs—and a T-shirt Aaron had let me borrow. Then I shot off another text to AJ, letting him know it looked like I wouldn't be able to get there until tomorrow at the earliest. Once I'd taken care of that, I slipped my phone into my pocket and headed downstairs with equal parts apprehension and intrigue.

The door to Barry's room was open, the space beyond empty, which meant they were both downstairs. I wasn't sure I'd be able to stomach seeing him with his hands on her. I'd suffered through seeing it for two years during high school, not to mention the ten years since then that I'd thought about it. It hadn't been easy, but I'd done it because I'd assumed Hannah had been happy. Now that I knew she wasn't?

Now that I knew she thought Barry was an asshole and was only with him out of convenience? The gloves were coming off. Hannah deserved so much better than my jackass of a brother, and I wasn't going to stop until she believed it.

The smell of coffee greeted me even before I rounded the corner into the large kitchen. My eyes immediately sought out Hannah, finding her leaning against the counter where the coffeemaker was. She looked hot as hell, even in a T-shirt and a modest-length skirt. Neither did anything to hide her subtle curves, and I longed to peel each piece off her body. Longed to finally see what I'd only fantasized about for so long. When I was done with my slow perusal of her body, I lifted my gaze to her eyes, finding her staring at me—cataloguing me much the same as I'd done to her. When our eyes met, she smiled—just a tiny curve of her lips, but it was enough. Part of me had worried I'd overstepped last night. Worried she'd be pissed at me, and that had been why she'd gone to Barry's room. But her smile set me at ease.

It felt like we were the only two people in the room, but that wasn't the case, much as I'd like it to be. Aaron stood a few feet away, brow creased as he scrolled through something on his phone, and Barry sat at the island, guzzling some orange juice.

He drained the glass before slamming it on the counter, not even sparing Hannah a glance as he demanded, "Banana, get me some more OJ."

Hannah shook her head and finally tore her eyes from me to glance his way. "What?"

I cut in before he had a chance to repeat his order, my hands curling into fists at my sides. "Get it yourself. She's not here to wait on you."

"Nah, she loves doing stuff for me," he said, waving me off, then turned to Hannah. "Don't you?"

Hannah narrowed her eyes and opened her mouth—hopefully, to tell the prick off—but Aaron's sharp curse stole everyone's attention.

"Shit!" Aaron hurried over to the French doors that opened to the deck. "One of the collapsible doors on the boathouse blew open. The furniture's gonna get soaked!" He grabbed his shoes and started putting them on. "I should probably check to make sure the Jet Ski is secure, too. I need to run out—"

A loud beeping sounded from the open door to the basement at the other side of the kitchen. "Aaron! I need some help down here," Jessica yelled.

"Fuck." He ran a hand through his hair, glancing outside, then toward the basement door, finally settling on Barry.

Barry held his hands up with a snort. "Don't look at me. These are thousand-dollar loafers. There's no way I'm going out there." He jerked his chin in Hannah's direction. "Banana can go. She's not wearing anything nice anyway."

I narrowed my eyes at Barry, restraining myself from punching him square in the jaw. A quick glance at Hannah proved she'd heard his comment. She stared at the floor, picking at the hem of her T-shirt. Barry had no fucking idea what he had—Hannah could be wearing a goddamn potato sack and she'd look gorgeous.

"You'd seriously send her out there by herself?" I asked as calmly as I could considering I wanted to strangle him with my bare hands.

"What?" He shrugged. "She can handle it. She deals in blood and guts every fucking day. A little rain isn't gonna hurt her."

"It's fine." Hannah waved a hand and headed toward the French doors, her back straight. Determined. "I can go out there so the prince here doesn't dirty his pretty shoes. God forbid his socks get wet."

Without waiting for a response from anyone, she was out the door. With a mumbled curse, I grabbed my shoes, hurrying to put them on. I didn't want Hannah to get far without me.

"Here, take a walkie," Aaron said. "Call if you have problems. I'll have the other one with me downstairs."

"Thanks." I grabbed it from him and headed to the French doors. Before I left, I looked at my brother. "You're an asshole, you know that?"

Barry laughed, tipping his freshly refilled glass of orange juice at me, sitting like a fucking king while the rest of us busted our asses. "So they tell me."

I slammed the door behind me and hustled into the pelting rain, jogging down the steps to the dock leading to the boathouse. Hannah was at the Jet Ski by the time I got to her, securing one side that had broken free in the storm. She was soaked to the bone, her T-shirt plastered against her body, and I had to force myself to look away so we could get this done as quickly as possible. Less than two minutes, and it already looked like she'd taken a dip in the lake.

It wouldn't be so bad if it were just some heavy rain, but the lightning was what concerned me. Just as the thought went through my mind, a sharp bolt flashed simultaneously with the rolling boom of thunder.

"Go in the boathouse," I yelled to be heard over the rain. "I've got this."

"It's faster if both of us work on it."

I tightened my jaw, irritated as hell that we were arguing about this when she was out here in the middle of a fucking lightning storm. "I don't care if it's faster. You'll be safer inside." I took the rope from her hands then jerked my chin in the direction of the boathouse. "Go. Please."

She huffed, wiping rain from her face. "Fine, but I'll be inside moving all the heavy furniture by myself, then."

I blew out an exasperated breath. "Just go inside and wait for two minutes, all right? I'll be there in a sec, and we can do it together."

She narrowed her eyes, then mumbled something I couldn't catch. But she turned her cute little ass around and did as I'd asked, marching straight into the boathouse.

I secured the Jet Ski as quickly as possible, then hurried inside, afraid I'd find Hannah attempting to heft a couch all by herself. Fortunately, she was just dragging an Adirondack chair away from the edge of the slip and out of the way of the rain. Still, it irritated me that she hadn't waited for me.

"Dammit, Hannah, I said we could do it together." Before she could get the other chair, I grabbed it and moved it farther inside, then closed and secured the collapsible doors, shutting out the pelting rain.

"This isn't the first time I've had to move furniture by myself, Luke. I moved all of my stuff out of your brother's apartment completely alone when I left him. I can handle some patio furniture." She stood in front of one of the chairs, her arms crossed, eyes narrowed on me.

Because, of course, my shithead of a brother had never helped her, especially when she was moving out. If only she'd moved *on*, too, instead of yo-yoing back with him time and time again. "Maybe not, and I know you're perfectly capable. That doesn't mean you should have to."

She froze, her mouth open as if to argue, but she snapped it shut and conceded my point with a short, "Fine."

Great, ten minutes into the day and we were already curt with each other. Once we'd made sure the rest of the furniture had survived the open door, I glanced outside to assess the situation. The rain came down in sheets, so heavy we couldn't even see the house. Lightning illuminated the sky nearly constantly, and thunder shook the floor of the boathouse. If it were just me out here, I'd chance going out to get back to the house. But with Hannah beside me? No fucking way.

"Looks like we're stuck in here for a while," I said. "I can't even see the house from here."

"Crap."

"Anxious to get back to your boyfriend?"

"He hasn't been my boyfriend in a long time, but no. Not really."

"No? What about last night?"

"What about it?"

I shook my head, not sure if she was being purposefully obtuse or what. I'd been going crazy wondering about what had happened last night, and she acted like it was nothing. After opening a few doors, I found a laundry room tucked into the back and grabbed a couple beach towels from the cabinet in the corner.

"Here." I handed her a towel, using the other on my hair. "We can toss our clothes in the dryer."

"And sit around in what?"

I held up a towel, raising an eyebrow. Her cheeks flushed as she glanced around, clutching the towel to her chest. Tipping my head toward the laundry room, I said, "Go ahead and change in there."

She headed to where I gestured, and I used the time to strip myself, peeling off my soaking wet T-shirt and jeans and trying not to think about the fact that there was only a door blocking me from a naked Hannah. Though, if I thought the towel would deter those fantasies, I was dead fucking wrong. She came out a couple minutes later, the beach towel so big it covered her from under her arms to mid-calf. Didn't matter. All it would take was one flick of my finger before that piece of fabric pooled at her feet.

Shaking my head, I walked around her, carrying

my jeans and T-shirt into the laundry room before tossing them in with hers.

I found her sitting primly on the couch, her shoulders curved in. "Are you cold? You want another towel?"

She glanced up at me, her eyes taking a path down my bare chest and stopping somewhere near the vicinity of my cock, barely hidden by the thin towel wrapped around my waist. Said cock twitched at her attention, the action no doubt noticeable. But who the fuck cared anyway? I'd made my desires known last night.

"Um, no thanks. I'm okay."

I took the seat next to her, my body completely aware of the fact that a nearly naked Hannah was six inches away. And as much as I wanted to use that to my advantage and show her what she'd been missing these last however many years, I had to know about last night. "Did you sleep in his room?"

She snapped her head in my direction, her lips parted. "Is that what this is about? Why you followed me out here when I could have handled tying off the Jet Ski?"

"I followed you because I care about you, and I wasn't about to let you wander out here by yourself. You lived on the island nearly your whole life—you know exactly how fast the storms can change." I raised an eyebrow. "What would you have done if I'd stormed out by myself?"

She narrowed her eyes, pursing her lips. Then she blew out a deep sigh. "I'd have followed you."

"Because you think I'm not capable of doing it on my own?"

"No, because you're just reckless enough to get yourself killed on the water. And I…" She picked at the hem of the towel, ducking her head before looking back at me. "I wouldn't want that to happen."

I reached out and brushed a loose piece of hair back from her face. "Where'd you sleep last night, Hannah?"

"It shouldn't matter."

"It matters to me. I thought that'd be pretty obvious after last night."

She shrugged. "I figured last night was the alcohol talking."

With a laugh, I said, "Two beers don't even get me buzzed. So, no, that was Sober Luke talking, and he meant every word." But hell, maybe she'd been drunk? She hadn't seemed it—tipsy, yes. But not so drunk that she hadn't been aware of what was happening. Then again, what the hell did I know? I hadn't seen Hannah drunk in a decade. "What about you?"

She bit her lip and shook her head. "I was tipsy but not out of control. I know what I said. Being sober doesn't change any of it."

"No? Then why didn't I find you in my bed when I came upstairs?"

Lifting a shoulder, she dropped her gaze. "I didn't think you were serious."

Was this girl for real? I huffed out a laugh. "I've been serious about it for a long damn time, Hannah."

"I didn't know." Licking her lips, she brought her

eyes back to my face, glancing down to my lips before meeting my eyes. "I slept on the chair. I wasn't in Barry's bed."

"Why not?"

"He's not what I want."

What I really wanted to ask was what, exactly, she wanted, but something told me even she didn't know. Not yet. Instead, I shifted closer to her, allowing my thigh to brush along hers. When she pressed against it, maintaining contact, I took that as a good sign. Slipping an arm behind her on the couch, I turned toward her, lifting a piece of her ponytail and rubbing it between my fingers. "Did you mean it last night?"

She mimicked my position, turning toward me and lifting her knee up just enough to rest it on top of my thigh, parting her legs enough that the towel pulled taut. My cock twitched, thinking about what she hid beneath that towel, how easy it'd be to slide my fingers up the inside of her thighs… Hannah tipped her head ever-so-slightly toward my hand, bringing my eyes up to hers. The move elongated her neck, making me want to run my nose, followed by my tongue, along the delicate skin.

Her eyes fluttered as I brushed my thumb along her jaw. "Mean what?"

I took a moment to study her. Goose bumps covered her arms, her breath came in soft pants, and the material of the beach towel did nothing to hide the hard points of her tits. Hannah was turned on, and I felt like I was ten feet tall. I leaned closer, finally giving in and letting my nose run along the length of her neck. Breathing in the scent that was pure Hannah. Sunshine and water—like a summer day.

Against her ear, I whispered, "When you said no one's ever made you scream…"

"Yes," she breathed.

"Never?" I moved my mouth to her neck, brushing my lips along the column in featherlight strokes. "You gonna let me between those gorgeous legs to try?"

She groaned, tilting her head farther to the side, allowing me more space to kiss. "*Jesus*."

"Is that a yes? All I need is a yes from you, sunshine, and then I'll try for hours if you'll let me." I pulled back, needing to look in her eyes when she answered. Needing to see for myself if this was something she wanted.

She bit her lip, her chest and cheeks flushed and so fucking gorgeous. Then she met my eyes and said, "Yes, Luke."

Jesus Christ, there was no hope for me after those two whispered words. Not with the almost desperate way she said them. I groaned, cupping her face in my hand before I covered her mouth with mine. Unable to wait another second, I slipped my tongue inside, moaning when she met me stroke for stroke. She wrapped her fingers around my forearm, clutching me to her. She tasted like heaven and hell all rolled into one—the most beautiful, forbidden temptation, and I was tired of denying myself.

With my mouth on hers, I pushed her back to recline against the arm of the couch and settled between her legs, pressing my aching cock against her. "Jesus, Hannah. You feel how hard you make me?"

She bucked against me. "*Yes.*"

I kissed my way down her body, brushing my lips across her collarbones before dipping to where she'd tucked the towel against her chest. Taking the material between my teeth, I glanced up at her with raised eyebrows, waiting for her to stop me. Waiting for her to do anything to keep me from pulling that material away and finally exposing her to me completely. When she dipped her chin in acknowledgment, I couldn't stop the groan that rumbled in my chest. Couldn't even pause as I tugged the material with my teeth, already brushing the towel aside with my hands to uncover my present underneath.

And holy fucking shit, if it were possible, Hannah Fedele was even more stunning than my fantasies had given her credit for. The softest, subtlest curves in the tiniest package I'd ever seen. Just as she moved an arm toward her breasts, I dipped down, sucking a hardened nipple into my mouth, deep enough to make her groan as her hands changed course and flew to my hair.

Pulling away, I blew on the tip, looking up at her. "Don't you dare cover yourself up from me. I've waited twelve fucking years for this. If we had more time, I'd spend an hour just staring. You're fucking gorgeous."

With wide eyes, she looked at me, mouth parted. Amazed. She looked amazed, like she'd never heard the words before. "Come here. Let me kiss you again."

"More of that later. Right now, I'm on a mission." I slid off the couch and knelt on the floor in front of her, gripping her by the ass to tug her toward the edge of the cushion. I wanted to press kisses to every inch of her body, wanted to lick her up one side and down the other. But right then, I couldn't think of anything but having her pussy against my tongue. My mouth actually watered at the thought, needing so desperately to taste her.

But Hannah was shy, if the way she tipped her knees in was any indication. She still wanted it—that much was clear by the subtle rolling of her hips—but something held her back. So rather than dive in face first like I wanted, I ran a finger from her clavicle, down between her breasts, around her belly button. Then I shifted direction, going down the seam of her thighs, so close to her pussy, but not quite close enough.

With each pass, Hannah inched her legs open a little more as if seeking my fingers, until finally, she was spread completely. She was wet as hell, the inside of her thighs glistening with her arousal, and her little clit peeked out at me, just begging for my tongue. She tossed her head to the side, lip tight between her teeth as she tried to contain her moans. It was no use, though. They filled the space around us, loud enough to be heard over the roaring of the storm outside. Oh yeah. I was going to make her scream, all right.

"You want this, don't you?" I asked, pressing a kiss to her inner thigh. So close to where I wanted to be. "Want me to finally make you come? Make you scream?"

"God, yes, Luke. Please."

"Are you going to let me?"

"Let you—"

I licked a line straight up the length of her slit, sucking her clit between my lips. I groaned against her at the same time a gasp fell from her mouth.

"Oh, Luke, don't—" She broke off on a moan as I flicked against her with my tongue.

Pulling back, I replaced my mouth with my fingers, rubbing tight circles around her clit. "Christ, you taste even better than I thought you would."

I dove back in, fixing my mouth to her, positively devouring her. She held my head in her hands the whole time, as if she couldn't decide if she wanted to push me away or pull me closer. And when she started chanting my name in a breathy, desperate way, it was too much. I tugged the towel from my hips, letting it pool on the floor as I gripped my cock with one hand. With my other, I slid two fingers into her pussy, groaning at how tight she was. I fucked her at the same pace I used on the fist wrapped around my erection, wishing with everything that it was my cock instead of my fingers deep inside her. She had me so worked up, I was about thirty seconds from blowing my load all over my hand. I needed her to come, and I needed it right fucking then.

I worked a third finger into her at the same time I gripped the base of my cock, attempting to stave off my orgasm. Through gritted teeth, I said, "Come on, sunshine. Come on my tongue. Let me taste it."

"Oh God, Luke. *Luke*."

I sucked her clit into my mouth, fluttering my tongue against it until she did exactly as I promised her and came with a scream. Her body bowed off the couch, her fingers tightening in my hair as she rolled her hips against me. I lightened my tongue to bring her down, even as I quickened the strokes against my cock until I was right on the edge, as desperate to come as she'd been.

When she finally relaxed her grip on my head, her entire body going boneless, I pulled back and rose on my knees as my balls pulled tight, the orgasm roaring through me like a freight train. With her name a groaned exhalation, I came against her stomach, rope after rope painting her flawless skin.

As the last wave shuddered through me, I glanced up, taking in her dropped mouth, her wide eyes, and silently cursed myself. What was I thinking, shooting my come all over her? Jesus Christ. "Sorry," I said with a shake of my head. "I shouldn't have done that, but licking your pussy got me too worked up."

She blinked at me, staring openmouthed. "You… you *liked* doing that?"

I huffed out a laugh even as I used my discarded towel to wipe the evidence of exactly how much I liked it from her stomach. "I fucking loved it." Once we were both cleaned up, I tossed the towel to the side and braced myself over her, brushing my lips against hers. "And I can't wait to do it again."

chapter four

HANNAH

AGAIN. He wanted to do that *again*. I wasn't the most experienced girl in the world—my only sexual experiences had sadly been with Barry—but that couldn't be normal. Barry had always complained about how long it took me to orgasm, about the taste and the…*oh God*, the smell. He would only do *that* if I'd showered first, and even then, he'd never been patient enough to make me come. I'd apparently been missing out. Luke had gotten worked up enough to need to jack off afterward, had enjoyed doing something to me so much that he came all over my stomach. My God was that hot.

Luke was still staring at me, still leaning in close. Still so gloriously naked. I had no idea where to look—those stunning blue eyes, as bright as the sky on a summer day, all the ink decorating his body, his soft, puffy lips, shining in the light with evidence of what he'd just done to me. Every inch of him intrigued me, aroused me. I wanted more. I wanted to run my palms over his body, wanted to stroke his cock and watch it harden in my hands because of what I was doing to him. I wanted so much.

"What's up, sunshine?" he asked, running a finger down the side of my face. "What are you thinking so hard about?"

Fear of being told no, of being rejected by him even after he'd gone down on me with such passion, turned my blood cold. What we were doing—what was happening between us—was a betrayal to someone he saw as family. I was okay with my part in that—if Barry never forgave me, I'd deal with the fallout. We hadn't been healthy together in years, and I'd finally come to terms with the fact that all contact needed to end. But Luke? Barry was practically his brother. They were family. And I...

I was going to destroy that.

"What are we—"

"Luke or Hannah." A staticky voice that sounded like Aaron burst into the room, making me jump and tug my discarded towel around myself. "You two okay?"

Luke rubbed my knee before stretching to grab a walkie-talkie device, smiling as he brought it to his lips. "We're good. Jet Ski secure, furniture saved, and door closed again. Just waiting out the lightning."

"I think it's passed," Aaron said. "I can see the boathouse again from the porch. Why don't you two come on back? I'll have hot coffee and blankets waiting."

"Will do." Luke set down the device, still watching me. "Time to go back to reality. But don't think I'm done with you yet."

"We can't…" I took a deep breath, reaching for him. "The others can't know. Not yet."

He sighed but didn't argue, brushing his fingers over my cheek instead. "Whatever you need."

"We just need to be subtle."

"Then we'll be subtle." He placed the softest, sweetest kiss on my lips, sending shivers up my spine in the process. "Much as I hate to cover you up, I'll go grab our clothes."

I sagged as he walked to the laundry room. Reality meant dealing with Barry and the fallout when he discovered what Luke and I had done. Because he would find out eventually, even though this was probably just something for the weekend. A distraction from real life.

That thought made my stomach drop, but there was no denying it. According to Barry, Luke wasn't exactly known for his relationship stamina, and I lived two hours off the island.

We had no future together, but we had chemistry. And I was willing to take what I could get of him. For once, I was going to be the selfish one.

———

Luke did not understand the meaning of the word subtle. After our private adventure in the boat house, we'd come back to join the rest of the group, an unspoken sort of understanding between us that we couldn't do anything like that again. Unspoken and not agreed on, apparently. He wouldn't stop staring at me. And not just any stare, *that* stare. The same look he'd given me when we'd been alone. And naked. And he'd dropped down between my legs.

God, just thinking about that look had me growing so hot and wet for him. Seeing it? Feeling the intensity of that look on his face? I was about to combust right there in Aaron and Jessica's kitchen.

"How about pizza for lunch?" Jessica asked from her side of the kitchen island. "I've got all the stuff to make homemade ones."

"So long as Hannah makes her own," Barry said. "She puts gross stuff on it."

"Pineapple is not gross," I said, rolling my eyes when Jessica looked my way.

"We can do individual crusts," she said, shooting me a wink. "And I've got a can of crushed pineapple we can use for toppings."

"Sounds good, babe," Aaron said as I mouthed a silent thank you to her. "Want some help?"

"Banana can help," Barry said right before he threw an arm around my shoulders and tugged me into his side. "She loves doing all that domestic shit."

Whether the burn in my chest was humiliation or fury, I could no longer tell. I shoved Barry off me. "Quit calling me Banana. But yes, Jessica. I'd love to help."

She glared at Barry before giving me a sympathetic smile. "I've got the dough in the basement freezer. Do you mind grabbing a few while I collect the rest of the ingredients?"

"No problem."

"See?" Barry said with a laugh. "Let the womenfolk do the cooking. Where's your biggest TV, Aaron? I think there's a race on."

If Jessica's glare was any indication, Barry should probably watch his back. She was definitely in the Barry-is-an-asshole camp.

I headed down the stairs, happy to be away from Barry's jackassery. Thrilled, really. He was ruining my post-Luke-between-my-thighs buzz. I needed to deal with his assumptions that we were still somehow together, and I needed to do it soon. I hated every time he said the nickname he'd refused to let me grow out of, and I didn't want his hands on me. We were going to have to have a conversation, one I'd have to initiate. Dammit.

The room with the freezer was shadowy, the only light coming from a small window at the back. I ran my hand all over the wall by the door, but I couldn't find the light switch. It wasn't too dark to see, so I headed right for the upright freezer. There had to be a light inside of it—Aaron didn't seem the type to skimp on bells and whistles. But before I could open the door, someone grabbed me from behind.

"What—"

Luke's mouth meeting mine cut off my yelp. He gave me no reason to be scared, no time to think about how wrong this whole thing was. He grabbed me, took my mouth with his, and made me melt. He was such a good kisser—strong and forceful but not demanding. Rough but not painful. All his need was evidenced in his kiss. All his desire. For me.

The man made my knees weak with how much he seemed to want me.

"I hate to see him touch you," he said as he moved those sexy lips down to trail along my neck.

I gripped his shoulders, holding myself to him. "I hate it, too. I don't want his hands on me."

"No?" Luke grabbed my ass and pulled me right off the ground, spreading my legs around his hips as he pressed me against the freezer. "What do you want?"

I couldn't even fake my answer, couldn't pause for a second before blurting out, "You."

His smile was immediate, though his lips settled into a more serious line before I could even enjoy it. "I'm not going to share, sunshine. If you want me, you get me—all of me. But the same goes for you. No more Barry. No more sleeping in his room." He kissed my collarbone and gripped my ass harder. "If you're serious, you come to *mine*."

There was no way I could resist him. "Okay."

———

One dry hump in the basement that only added to the tension between Luke and me, five bites of the pizza Jessica had made, and two hours of watching cars drive in a circle was enough for me. Luke had disappeared upstairs, claiming he needed a nap. Aaron and Jessica were watching the race in the family room, and Barry…

Barry was getting a clue.

"Hannah, you can't be serious."

"I am." I crossed my arms and leaned back against the kitchen counter. "We're through. And not the back-and-forth through we were doing last year. We're done. Permanently."

"Right," he scoffed, rolling his eyes. "And what are you going to do when you crack the next time because your job is so hard?"

God, I hated him. Hated that he threw my weaknesses at me every time I tried to put space between us. "I'll get a cat."

He nodded, still looking as if he didn't believe me. "Okay, fine. You want this over? It's over. I'm perfectly capable of finding another way to get my dick wet. You can enjoy rubbing your pussy all alone." He slammed his glass down, the only real sign of how pissed I'd just made him. "Have fun sleeping on the couch in the basement, and don't you dare take anything from my room that isn't yours."

I took a deep breath once he left the room, unsure if I was more afraid or excited. While Barry and I hadn't been together as a couple in a long time, I still felt guilty because of Luke. The conversation of us being done for good had needed to happen. Hell, if I was being honest with myself, it had needed to happen years ago.

But he was right about the work thing—I tended to call him when I was worn out. When my emotions were raw and I just needed someone to hold me. To help me put myself back together. That was how we'd always ended up in bed together again—my job skinned me alive, and the only cure for me was physical contact with someone. Affection. Intimacy. Something to make me forget the death and the pain. I needed to be stronger, to learn to cope on my own. I couldn't fall into that trap again.

Without thinking about it, without intentionally making the decision to go to Luke, I headed up the stairs. Barry's door sat open, but Luke's was closed. It didn't matter. I knew he was in there, that he was waiting for me.

I was tired of waiting.

My knuckles hit the panel of wood once before it swung inward, and Luke was on me. He yanked me inside, wrapping me in his strong arms and holding me to his chest. And for the first time in a long time, I felt safe and cared for.

"What took you so long?" he asked, breathing into my neck as if he needed my scent to survive. "I thought you might've changed your mind."

I pressed myself into his arms and shook my head, not wanting words. Not wanting anything but him and me and bare skin. I could tell he wanted the same simply by the way he pressed his hardening cock into my hip. There was no hiding that growing desire. No ignoring it either.

I pushed away from him, loving how he let me

go, how he let me make the decision of what was next without a fight. I hated the confusion on his face, though. I wasn't rejecting him. Not even close. He needed to know that.

I took another step back, gave him a smile, and then I stripped. Not slow like a tease and not fast like we were in a hurry. No, I stripped like I would on any night. I pulled my shirt over my head and unhooked my bra, letting both fall to the floor. My skirt and underwear came next, pooling at my feet as Luke watched, his eyes sliding over every inch of skin as I exposed myself to him. As he stood stock-still, pure energy harnessed into his big body. Ready to explode. Waiting for the ignition switch to click.

So I clicked it.

"I'm here," I said, my voice soft but firm. "I'm here, and I want you. Just you."

His groan made my knees shake, but his strong arms wrapping around me again held me up. Kept me safe and warm. "Jesus, Hannah. Can't believe this is real. Can't believe you're giving me this beautiful body."

"I still can't believe you want me."

He captured my mouth without another word, spinning me and laying me back on his bed. I climbed up the length of it as he watched, as he stripped for me.

"Can't believe I'd want you?" He shook his head as if he couldn't believe my words. "I've ached for this for twelve fucking years. Twelve *years*. And it's been worth every second of denial if this is my reward." He crawled over me, his heavy cock hanging down all hard and ready. His hands finding every bit of flesh he could as he moved between my thighs. "But now you're here, and you're mine. And I'm not letting you go."

I wanted to believe him, wanted to think that we'd get our happily ever after and everything would be okay. But the reality was that this was probably a weekend fling. Something to look back on when I was alone in the city, something to cherish. And I was going to have to be okay with that.

"Want you," I said just before I bit down on his neck. His body jerked, his hips rubbing against my thigh. "Want to feel you inside me."

He ground his cock against my hip, groaning softly before rolling off to the side. "Soon, sunshine. Let me make you come first. Make you so wet you'll be able to take my cock."

His fingers were soft and seeking as they slid to where I was swollen for him. He teased me with gentle strokes and easy flicks before ramping up the motions. Harder, faster, working his thumb over my clit as he plunged two fingers inside. I arched and bit my lip, writhing under him. Pinned in place by his weight on one side. That only added heat to the moment.

Something about knowing it was Luke on top of me, about watching those eyes flick between mine and where his hand disappeared between us, made everything burn that much brighter. He wasn't the man I should have been with, but I couldn't resist him. And to be honest, I didn't want to try.

Luke was thorough in his attention, such a giver. He lapped at my nipples, tugging the hardened flesh between his teeth as he added a third finger inside of me. The pull, the tiny bit of pain, the tight stretch of him filling me—it was all too much. I came with a quiet yelp, Luke covering my mouth with his to silence the worst of it as my body locked down. I was fine with that—I kissed him deeply, shaking underneath him, stroking his tongue with mine to keep us connected. And when he finally broke away, when he trailed his lips along my jaw, I whispered his name like a chant, unable not to claw at his shoulders, to try to pull him closer.

He moved back up and kissed me again, sliding his tongue against mine in a desperate sort of pace. He was so turned on, so ready for me. That desire in him was another turn-on, and I longed to make him mine. To feel him move inside of me. To make him come with my body alone.

So I pushed him over and rolled with him, wrapping my legs around his hips as I bit down on his bottom lip. Sitting on his hips as I dragged my lips to his ear and whispered, "It's your turn to scream *my* name."

chapter five

OVER THE PAST twelve years, I'd had hundreds of dreams that'd played out just like this. Hannah ending up under or over me, naked and willing. *Wanting.* Her lips whispering my name, her nails scratching down my back, her legs spread just for me. She'd been the star of my teenage wet dreams…was still the star even a decade later. But my fantasies hadn't quite gotten it right. Before this morning, I didn't know she had a tiny birthmark on her inner thigh. Could never have predicted the exact sound of her moans when she came. Couldn't have known how amazing she'd taste, how perfect she'd feel. How desperate but reluctant she'd be…

She was the most gorgeous woman I'd ever seen, and she somehow didn't see it. That asshole stepbrother of mine had obviously done a number on her, making her question everything about herself. Making her shy and hesitant, uncomfortable in her own skin. I hated it, hated *him.*

I shoved those thoughts away, not wanting to think about them together. Every shitty thing he'd ever done to her just meant I'd work that much harder to show her how beautiful she was, how amazing, how lucky I was that she'd chosen me. I'd spend every day for months reminding her, if she'd let me. And since she was here, naked and in my bed, I took that as a good sign that she wanted this just as much as I did. Wanted to hear me scream *her* name.

I cupped the back of her head, pulling her face toward me and capturing her bottom lip between my teeth, giving a quick tug. "Before we get to me, I need another taste." With my hands on her ass, I guided her up my body, getting her as far as my stomach before she froze.

She pushed against my chest, sitting back and giving me an amazing view of her tits. "Another taste of what?"

I smiled, slipping my hand between us and not stopping until I reached her pussy. As soon as my fingers hit her clit, she groaned, dropping her head down between her shoulders, her hair tickling my chest.

"This," I said, pulling my hand back and sucking my fingers into my mouth as I hummed. "Jesus, you taste good. I could eat you for every meal and still not get enough."

"You don't have to do that. I know it's not… anyone's favorite thing."

"You think I don't *like* it? My reaction should be pretty obvious, sunshine." Even though she sat too far up on my stomach for contact, my cock still reached for her, the tip weeping. "Go ahead and feel. Feel how hard the taste of you makes me. See how much I want you to sit on my face so I can lick you all up."

Without hesitation, she did as I suggested, slipping her hand behind her until those dainty fingers wrapped around my cock. I groaned, my eyes fluttering closed before I snapped them open, wanting to see her face the first time she touched me. Her eyes were wide, her bottom lip caught between her teeth as she stroked from root to tip, feeling me, studying me…

"Hard as fuck, all because of you." I thrust my hips into her fist, reaching up to cup one of her breasts, the position she was in pushing them toward me. But they were too far away. I wanted them in my mouth. Wanted to memorize every fucking inch of her with just my tongue.

"C'mere." I tugged her down, bringing her nipple straight to me so I could engulf it in my mouth. She moaned, her hand slipping higher on my cock, her fist just around the head as I lapped at her tits, trying not to go off as she gave me a clumsy hand job.

With a hand firm on her ass, I guided her lower body higher until I finally had to relinquish my hold on those beautiful breasts. Until she was sitting high on my chest, so near where I wanted her to be. Close but not nearly close enough.

Before I could scoot her up any farther, she released my cock and settled her hands between her legs, blocking my view of her pussy. "What do you think you're doing here?"

"Trying to get a taste." I shot her a grin, squeezing her ass. "Why don't you come on up here and ride my face?"

She shook her head, her face flaming. "I've never— I can't—"

"You can. Just forget about what I'm doing. Stroke my cock. You wanted to make me scream your name, remember?"

"Luke," she said, her voice almost a whine. Frustrated. And turned the hell on, if the slow rocking of her hips was any indication. "Not like this. I want you inside me."

"Oh, sunshine, it'd take a force of God to keep me from burying myself in your pussy. But first, I need to get you soaking wet so you can take my cock." I slid a hand up the inside of her thigh, bypassing her blocking hands, and ran a single finger through her slit. "Come up here and let me."

Hands braced on my chest, she bit her lip, uncertainty written all over her face even as she rocked against my circling finger. She wanted something more, and I was happy to give it to her.

"If you don't like it this way, we can stop. Anytime you want. Promise." I raised an eyebrow and waited for her to decide. Trying to mask how desperately I wanted my tongue on her again. Because, in the end, it was her decision, and I needed her to pick it because *she* wanted it, not just because I did.

Finally, she gave a stilted nod. "But I don't know what I'm doing. You're going to have to show me."

With a grin, I rubbed circles around her clit and coaxed her higher with one hand on her ass. Guided her until her knees were on either side of my head, and she held herself above me, her pussy open and swollen and wet. Just inches from my face, and so fucking obscene. Obscene and begging for my tongue. "Reach back and stroke my cock."

She immediately did as I said, arching her back to grab my cock, the position only spreading her wider. Offering up more of her to me.

"Jesus, Hannah. You've got the prettiest little pussy I've ever seen, you know that? C'mere and let me have another taste."

She shuddered over me as she pumped me in slow, fumbling strokes. "I don't know…" she breathed, shaking her head. "I don't think I can—"

"You know what I think?" I asked, the scent of her arousal so close it made my mouth water. "I think you'll be riding my tongue in two minutes flat."

And then I anchored her with my hands on her waist and lifted my head toward her, taking a long swipe through her slit with my tongue. "Mmm… love how you taste. Love how wet you get for me." I suctioned her clit between my lips, flicking against it with my tongue. Remembering what had gotten her off in the boathouse, but wanting to try other things too. Wanting to try everything with her.

"Oh God…" She relaxed in increments, her body growing pliant under my hands as she lowered herself by centimeters and started rocking her hips against my mouth, her grip on my cock clumsy and stuttered. My two-minute estimate was off by a whole fucking lot.

I hummed against her, loving how much she was getting into this, despite her initial hesitation. She moaned in response, quickly cutting the sound off by pressing her lips together as she shot a worried look toward the door. Toward the sounds going on beyond it—Aaron and Jessica and Barry talking downstairs, their voices carrying up the steps. Then she looked down at me, all the while still rocking against my mouth, still pressing her pussy to me, silently begging me not to stop. Maybe the thought of getting caught turned my girl on…

Gripping her ass in my hands, I held her tight to me. Wanting her closer, wanting to *devour* her. After so long of being deprived of her, I couldn't get enough. Would *never* get enough. Not when it came to Hannah.

Before long, she let go of my cock to grip the headboard, rocking over my face with abandon. Her whimpers telling me just how close she was to her release. I let my fingers trail between her cheeks, not breaching her back entrance, but keeping a teasing presence there. She shivered, her eyes wide as she bit her lip and looked down at me. Like she wasn't sure she should like that. Like she wasn't sure she was supposed to.

Fuck that.

Not wanting her to question anything that felt good, I let my fingers press a little harder and sucked her clit between my lips. She shuddered over me, a sharp cry leaving her lips before she stifled it with the back of her hand. And then she was coming all over my face, her hand gripping in my hair, hips rolling.

As long as I lived, I would never get enough of feeling and seeing Hannah come.

I didn't even let her ride out her orgasm before I had her flipped over on the bed, too desperate to feel her around me. Fucking finally. In two seconds flat, I had on the condom I'd set out earlier in hopeful anticipation and had her parted legs hooked over my elbows so she was spread open and waiting. Ready.

And then I pushed into the most perfect heaven I'd ever felt.

"Jesus *Christ*, Hannah." I groaned, dropping my head and willing myself patience. Forcing myself to pause and let her get used to me, even though only the head of my cock sat nestled inside her tight pussy.

"Luke—" She gasped as I pressed farther into her, working so desperately to go slow.

Hannah was petite under normal circumstances, but compared to me, she was fucking *tiny*. If I rammed my cock into her like I wanted to, I'd only hurt her, despite the fact that her wetness still coated my mouth, made the insides of her thighs shiny. I watched where she was open wide around me, taking my cock inch by inch, her moans spurring me on, until finally, *finally*, she took everything I gave her.

"Holy fuck, I never thought—" I shook my head, the reality of being with her so much better than even my best fantasies. I pulled back nearly all the way, holding still until just the tip sat inside, and then I pushed deep, groaning as I watched her pussy swallow my cock. "You feel so fucking good. How is this real?"

"I don't know, but please don't stop."

"Never." Abandoning the view of her spread around my cock, I braced myself on the mattress and leaned over her, capturing her mouth in a kiss, needing her lips on mine. She reached up, cupping my face as she met my tongue stroke for stroke, groaning as she tasted herself on me.

"Told you," I whispered against her. "Best dessert I've ever had."

"Luke—" She broke off on a moan as her pussy fluttered around me, her hands clutching me to her. "So close."

"Yeah, you are. I can feel you. Jesus, your pussy squeezes my cock so tight." I rolled my hips, grinding against her clit with every pass, desperate to feel her come around me. Desperate to finally let myself go.

"I'm—" With a whimper, she dug her nails into my ass, keeping me seated deep inside her as she rocked her hips against me. "I think I'm going to come."

"You gonna be quiet for me so we don't get caught?" I nuzzled her neck, capturing her earlobe between my teeth while grinding my hips against hers. "Or do you like that idea? Like the thought of him walking in and seeing how a real man treats this perfect little pussy? So we can show him how you drip down my chin and soak my cock?"

"Oh God." Hannah arched her back and gasped, her entire body going taut before she moaned low and deep, the sound barely caught between my lips as she came around me. Unable to wait another second, I pumped into her with fast strokes, desperate to come. To go off inside her after twelve long years of only dreaming about it.

"*Fuuuuck*," I groaned into her mouth, thrusting as deep as I could, a full-body shudder working its way through my limbs as my release claimed me.

"We should have done this years ago." Hannah's fingers traced soft lines up and down my back as I struggled to hold myself above her, trying to remember how to fucking *breathe*. Jesus, it'd never been like this before. Ever. Somehow, I knew it'd be different with her, but this… This, I hadn't been expecting.

As much as I wanted to pump into her again, my cock already getting ideas of going once more, I gripped the base and pulled out, discarding the condom in the wastebasket by the bed. And then I collapsed on my back, immediately tucking her into my side with my hand firm on her ass. She came without hesitation, snuggling in and resting her face on my chest, her leg hooked over mine.

Perfection.

Well, almost. There was the tiny detail of her being my brother's…girlfriend? Ex-girlfriend? I didn't know. It was something we needed to discuss, something we needed to figure out together. Real life would creep in eventually, but for that moment, I was content with Hannah in my arms, her fingers trailing up and down my chest, her satisfied breaths against my skin. Her cheek puffing against me as she smiled.

chapter six

THE WOMAN IN the bathroom mirror couldn't be me. Her smile was too big, her cheeks too rosy, and her hair was an absolute mess. Totally not me, and yet…

I pinched my cheek, trying hard to rein in my grin. Failing miserably because of the man waiting in the other room for me to come back to bed. Luke. He'd blown into my life just like the storm still raging outside, knocking everything out of whack and turning the world slightly upside down. Had I really had three orgasms in his bed? Had I honestly knelt over his face so he could…

I couldn't think about what he'd done without my cheeks flushing pinker and my pussy growing wet again. The man was amazing. And very possibly someone who wanted to be a part of my life.

Before I could even let my brain begin to deal with the complications of how that would work, Luke was behind me. Still naked. Still so handsome it hurt.

"I don't know why you're in here when you could be in bed. With me."

I leaned back into his arms, letting his warmth surround me. Forgetting for the moment all the logistics of him having a business in Temperance Falls and me living over two hours inland. "I was distracted by the awful bird's nest on my head. What did you do to my hair?"

"You're beautiful." He leaned down to bite along my neck, his hands coming up to grip and knead my breasts. His hips rolling into mine and proving how hard he was for me already. "And in case you forgot, I'm happy to show you again just how good I can treat this pussy."

"Again?" But he didn't answer me with words. No, Luke kicked my legs apart and bent me over the vanity, sliding a hand between us as he did.

"Again and again and again, as long as I've got breath, sunshine."

His fingers were so thick inside me as his thumb rolled over my clit. Less than a minute, and the man had me panting, arching, and writhing underneath him. It was as if he knew every one of my buttons, as if he'd somehow studied exactly how to get me off. He kept his eyes on me the entire time, kept his hand moving, teasing, thrusting inside of me until I came with a quiet groan right there against the counter.

Luke didn't miss a beat, drawing out every second of pleasure he could from me before grabbing his cock with his wet hand and stroking himself. I watched in the reflection, obsessed with the way he kept his eyes on my ass, at the roughness of his pulls. Witnessing him take his pleasure was something I hadn't thought would be so devastatingly hot, but it was. It totally was.

Wanting to help him, needing to see him reach that peak, I spun around. With a little hop, I was sitting on the edge of the counter, spreading my knees wide.

"Better?"

"Fuck, sunshine. Look at you all spread and swollen, still wet from my hands." He groaned loud and deep, his hand moving faster, eyes pressing closed for just a moment. "I want to drop to my knees right here and lick you up again." He leaned in to kiss me, his hand brushing against me with every stroke. Teasing me again. Every little grunt, every sigh or groan, had me dying for more.

"Remember in the boathouse," I whispered, leaning closer. Letting my voice drop. "Remember when you came on my stomach after giving me my first orgasm with a partner in years? All those ribbons of your come lying across my skin like some sort of marking?" I bit his ear in a teasing sort of tug. "That was the hottest thing I'd ever seen. Until now."

"Oh Jesus, Hannah."

"Look at how rough you are. How fast your hand moves." I reached out, running a finger down his bicep, palming his forearm as it jerked up and down. "I could never be that rough with you."

Still, I wanted him to have more than just his own hand. Wanted him to let me make him come. And I wanted to taste him the way he'd tasted me.

"But I can do other things." I shoved him back a step, dropping to my knees and swatting away his hand. Luke stared down at me, practically panting, his cock leaking right there in front of my face. So hard. So ready.

I leaned forward to kiss the tip, a moment of sweetness given to him before I opened my lips and took him deep inside. Swallowing around him. Luke grabbed my head, tangling his fingers in my hair as he moved me gently back and forth. As he rocked his hips into my mouth and back out again, fucking my face.

"Oh fuck, oh *fuck*. Should've known this mouth would be heaven. Just like every fucking inch of you."

I groaned, placing my hands on his thighs and bobbing faster, sucking harder. I was already so wet again, so hungry for him. I had no idea how we were going to make it through another two days without exposing our secret, but I didn't care. All I wanted, all I needed, was for Luke to come. I craved it.

I slipped a hand between my legs, teasing myself as Luke's movements became a little rougher, a little off rhythm. He was close. And I—

Luke grumbled something that sounded like a string of curses, his hips snapping faster. "Are you touching yourself, sunshine? You love the feel of my cock in your mouth that much? Does the taste of what you do to me make you needy?" He brought his hand to my lips as I stared up at him. His finger traced the edge, so sweet and soft. So gentle with me even as he fucked my face. As he took what I offered so he could get off.

"You're the hottest fucking thing I've ever seen." He thrust three more times before coming with a groan, pressing deep into my mouth as I swallowed everything down. As I came with my fingers buried inside myself and a muffled moan on my lips.

On his cock.

"Jesus H. Christ, Hannah. You're so fucking perfect for me." Luke picked me up, picked me up right off the floor, and wrapped my legs around his hips. He carried me the few feet across the bathroom to the stone shower, kissing me the entire way. Gripping my ass like he owned it until we reached the taps. With one hand, he turned on the water, adjusting the temperature until it was warm and steamy in the little alcove.

"Come on, sunshine. Let's get you cleaned up before we have to rejoin the rest of the group."

———

After our shower together—and Luke kneeling between my legs to make me come on his tongue one more time—we dried off and headed back to the land of the not-completely-obsessed-with-inappropriate-sex. For hours, we circled one another, staying away as much as possible as we socialized with the others and waited out the storm. Coming together whenever we thought no one would notice to brush hands or arms, though Luke preferred to run his palm over my ass if possible. I had to bite back a smile every time, knowing I could give us away. Wishing we could retreat back to our little bubble of just the two of us.

But that was not to be.

"We should watch a movie," Jessica said when the guys finally emerged from the TV room.

"That sounds good." Aaron wrapped his arms around her and kissed her neck, something that made my stomach lurch. Luke and I couldn't do that, not here. Not now. I caught his eye across the kitchen, noticing his frown, and knew he was thinking the same thing.

"The storm doesn't look as bad," Barry said, appearing at the opposite end of the kitchen. "Maybe we can actually escape to someplace cooler soon. No offense, Aaron."

"None taken." Aaron rocked Jessica, both looking pretty offended no matter what words were spoken.

"I don't know, I think this place is pretty great," Luke said, giving me a subtle wink. "Despite the storm, this has been one of the best weekends I can remember."

Jessica smiled as she looked from him to me and back. But that smile dropped when Barry laughed.

"You need to get out more, bro. Hopefully, we can make it to the reunion tomorrow night and get this over with. Banana and I left the island for a reason, and I, for one, am ready to get back to the city and the real nightlife."

"I'm with Luke," I said, drawing everyone's attention. "I've had a great day. Thank you, Jessica and Aaron. Your home is beautiful, and I've felt nothing but welcomed here."

Barry frowned as he looked my way, his eyes seeming to want to delve deeper. To figure out what was going on with me. I kept a smile on my face and stared right back, not flinching. Not backing down. Luke had made the last twenty-four hours as perfect as they could have been, and I wasn't about to let Barry take away that glow.

"You guys watch your movie," he finally said, still looking at me with something close to suspicion in his eyes. "I'm going to grab my computer and get some work done. You do have internet, right?"

Aaron sighed and nodded. "Yeah. Come on, you can set up in my office."

Within minutes, Jessica had one of the latest superhero movies on the big screen, popcorn in bowls spread out on tables, and the lights dimmed. But I couldn't pay attention to the plot. I was too busy staring at Luke, at the way his jeans pulled tight across his thighs. At the patterns of ink stamped along his forearms. So when he caught my eye and angled his head toward the door before he got up and headed toward the kitchen, I couldn't help but follow. I needed a moment alone with him even if it was just a few seconds.

I found Luke on the back porch watching the

rain fall, his arms stretched out against the railing, his back tense. He reminded me of a caged animal in that pose, something I hadn't been expecting.

I placed a hand on his shoulder, inching around to stand beside him. "What's wrong, Luke?"

"I meant it, you know. What I said in there." He grabbed my hand and pulled me into his arms. Clinging to me. Breathing me in with his face buried in my neck. "This has been one of the best days of my life, sunshine."

"Mine too." My admission came with a side of fear, though. Of worry. I curled myself into his hold, clutching his arms to me as we rocked with the pitter-patter of the rain on the roof. Wishing I could hang on to him every day but knowing that was a pipe dream. "What happens when it's time to go back to the real world?"

"We go back together." His words were so straightforward, so solid. So not doable.

"I live two hours away."

He leaned down to kiss my neck. "We'll make it work, Hannah. I promise."

But as his hands slipped under my clothes, as he rubbed up and down my back right there on the porch watching the rain, I worried.

Nothing could be as easy as his words implied. Life wasn't that simple or guaranteed. We had another two days for sure, which was more than I could have hoped for. After that...

Well, there was no after that yet. There was hope and want, but no plan. No certainty. No forever.

chapter seven

LUKE

IT'D BEEN HOURS—eleven, but who was counting?—since I'd last been inside Hannah. Sometime last night, it'd come to light that Barry had kicked Hannah out of his room when she'd talked to him yesterday, setting him straight about the fact that they were done. For good this time. Thank fucking God. But with the bridge to the mainland still flooded and keeping us all there, that'd meant she hadn't had a place to sleep. Since we'd both agreed to keep this thing between us under wraps for the time being, I couldn't exactly invite her to sleep with me. So I'd given her my room and gone to sleep in the basement.

Or that was what I'd told everyone.

Sometime around midnight, I'd snuck into the room, unable to deprive myself of her after going so long without. She'd welcomed me, spreading her legs wide as I'd slid into her bed, and then slid into the warm heaven of her pussy, cupping my hand over her mouth to keep her quiet, all the while whispering the multitude of things I'd wanted to do to her. Things I wanted to do to her right fucking now.

But it wasn't going to happen. At least, not for a while. Not when we were in the kitchen surrounded by Jessica and Aaron, Barry roaming around being an asshole somewhere close. I couldn't exactly pin her against the counter and bunny-fuck her like I wanted with all these witnesses. But, *Jesus*, I wanted. I was getting the shakes, like a junkie hungry for their next fix. It'd been too damn long since I'd felt her lips on mine, her fingernails digging into my ass, her breathy pleas begging me to go *faster, deeper, don't stop, never stop*. As if I could.

Twelve years had come and gone since I'd first set my sights on Hannah, my interest piquing with something more than the platonic relationship we'd had. Twelve years I'd filled with work and friends and other women, and yet the thing I'd looked forward to the most had been some damn emails, a few texts, and a phone call once in a while if I was lucky. Anything where I could get a glimpse into her life. Anything that told me she was happy. That she was fulfilled and satisfied, even if it meant it wasn't with me.

But all that contact had nothing on getting information from her in person. And it hadn't even been what she'd *said* as much as everything she hadn't. Her body language, her tired eyes the first night I'd seen her, how she'd curled into herself whenever Barry was around… She might love her job, but that was the only thing in her life that made her happy, all the while draining her.

Now, she sat at the small table in the breakfast nook, laughing at something Jessica said, not paying me any mind. Meanwhile, I couldn't look anywhere but at her. Her head was tossed back, her shiny pink lips spread in a smile…so fucking beautiful. Her concern over what we'd do tomorrow when it was time for her to go back to the city, when it was time for me to go back to the brewery, to reality, just meant I had to be transparent in my intentions. Hannah wasn't leaving Temperance Falls without knowing exactly what she meant to me—what she'd *always* meant to me. Now that I'd had her, now that I'd had a taste of what it'd be like to be with her? It'd take a damn force of nature to tear me away from her.

Despite the fact that she was my brother's ex-girlfriend.

"Word to the wise," Aaron said, breaking my trance. "Maybe try to be a little less obvious when Barry's around."

"Obvious about what?" I asked, not taking my gaze off Hannah, tracing my eyes over the column of her neck down to her chest, sure I could see the outline of her nipples through that shirt.

He snorted and leaned against the counter next to me. "Come on, man. She might be all the way across the room, but I'm surprised her clothes haven't spontaneously combusted with how hard you're eye-fucking her."

I slid him a look, but he held up his hands and shook his head. "No qualms from me. I've always thought the two of you would be better together than her and that jackass. No offense."

"Again, none taken." I couldn't care less if he called Barry every name in the book. Whatever he said would probably be true.

"So, what's the plan?" He elaborated when I raised my eyebrows in response. "You and Hannah."

I shrugged, hating the words even as I said them. "We thought it would be better not to make a big deal until after the weekend."

"How do you think that's going to go at the reunion tonight?"

"We'll see if we can make it there, I guess."

"Bridge is clear. I just got a message that the reunion is on."

I blew out a breath, knowing it was going to be the hardest test of all. Being stuck in a house with all kinds of rooms we could disappear into was one thing. Being in a crowded space with her and not having her pressed against me? Not letting everyone know she was the one I wanted? It'd be difficult as hell, but we'd get through. We had to.

"It'll go how it needs to go."

"Let me ask you something," Aaron said. "How long's it been since Barry's been back to the island? Been to visit your mom or stopped by the brewery?" The look he gave me said he already knew the answer.

Still, I said, "Never. He left and hasn't been back once. Until now."

Aaron hummed, tipping his chin down in a nod. "You wanna know what I think?"

My lips quirked at the sides. "I think you're going to tell me no matter what."

"You're right. Seems to me he doesn't deserve the loyalty you're somehow still giving him. Something to think about." He clapped his hand on my shoulder, then headed toward his wife and the woman who'd been my one true north for twelve years, the one I'd always kept in my sights even when I couldn't reach her.

I let his words sink in, not realizing how much I'd needed to hear them until they'd been spoken. It helped me come to the conclusion I should've come to long ago. Barry was an asshole who cared about no one but himself. Family was a foreign concept to him, something born of obligation instead of loyalty. He hadn't given me his in a long damn time—maybe ever.

It was time I stopped giving him mine.

————

I was sure this was a test. There was no other explanation for being forced to watch Hannah circle the room, laughing and talking with our classmates, many of whom we hadn't seen in ten years, while not being able to touch her.

With the bridge clear, I'd finally been able to go home and change out of the clothes I'd been recycling for two days. Unable to find a good excuse for her to come with me, we'd agreed to meet back up at the reunion. I'd gotten there early after swinging by the brewery to make sure things were running smooth. AJ had practically pushed me out the door, and because I'd been so eager to have Hannah in my sights again, I went without complaint. And then she'd walked into the school right on time, looking like sex on heels and nearly making me fall to my goddamn knees.

Her hair was pulled back in a fancy looking ponytail, her lips brushed in something bright pink and shiny, her eyes dark and sexy. But it was the dress that did me in. Painted on her like a second skin, it stopped mid-thigh and dipped low at her chest—so low I knew there was no way she was wearing a bra. The subtle shadow of her tits in the deep V had given me my first hard-on of the night, and it hadn't abated. The dress fit her like it'd been tailor-made for her, the pink pattern of it sparkling against the black backdrop. I wanted to rip it off her. Wanted to ruck it up against her waist, tug her panties to the side, and push into her snug little pussy, not stopping until we both got what we wanted. Until we were both breathing hard and sated, our names on each other's lips.

And that was why I'd walked around for the past two hours rocking serious wood behind the zipper of my dark jeans and hoping like hell the lighting hid my reaction to her. I just had to make it a little while longer, then I could make excuses, hoping Hannah did the same, and drag her back to my place.

That plan blew up in my face as I watched Barry

strut over to her, tossing an arm around her shoulders as she talked to a couple people I vaguely recognized. Despite the way she shrugged him off, shooting him a look, despite the talk she'd already had with him, he still pushed himself on her. Still pretended they were an item and everything was fine.

Fuck. That.

I wanted to go over and shove him off her, wanted to press her right up against me where she belonged. But Hannah didn't want to make a scene, so I stayed put, willing my feet to listen and not walk straight to her. Instead, I shot her a quick text. She ducked out from under Barry's arm again and lifted her phone, glancing once at the screen before she sought me out in the gymnasium. When she found me, I tilted my head toward the exit. Her only answer was a quirk of her lips and the slight dip of her chin. That was all I needed.

With determination, I strode out of the gym after excusing myself from a conversation I was barely a participant in. Everything about the high school was still the same, so I knew exactly where I was headed, hoping the janitor's closet on the far side of the school hadn't been turned into something else. We'd called it the Boner Box in high school because it'd been where couples—or not-couples—would go to get their rocks off in the middle of the school day. Not the flowers and candles Hannah deserved, but I needed to be with her right fucking then, needed to remind myself Barry no longer had a hold on her.

When I got to the door, I sent up a silent plea

as I turned the knob, blowing out a relieved breath when it opened with ease. I shot Hannah another text, letting her know where to find me. And then I waited.

A thousand heartbeats later, the knob turned before the door creaked open enough to show Hannah's silhouette backlit by the lights in the hallway. I didn't say anything as I yanked her into the room, shutting the door behind her and pressing her up against it.

"Luke? What—"

I cut off her question with my mouth, swallowing her broken moan. Reveling in the fact that she melted into my touch, sank into my body like it was where she belonged.

"Can't stand his fucking hands on you," I said, gripping her under the thighs and hauling her up against me. Even in heels, she barely came up to my chin, and I needed her closer. "I tried to wait, but I couldn't. I couldn't—"

"So don't." She wrapped her legs around me, pressing her pussy against where I was so hard and aching for her.

"Need to get you ready. Need to get you soaking wet, sunshine. That tiny little pussy has to be slicked up to take me, doesn't she?" I slid my hand down to cup her ass, not stopping until I touched her pussy from behind. Finding her both bare and wet, her thighs damp with her arousal. "*Fuck*, you've been walking around without any panties all night? So wet you're dripping down these beautiful thighs?"

She panted as I rubbed her clit. "I kept thinking of you as I got dressed, remembering how hard and fast your hand moved on your cock. I was so turned on, I tried to masturbate, but my fingers weren't enough. I needed yours. I've been waiting for you all night."

"Jesus Christ, how am I supposed to be gentle now? How am I supposed to do anything but fuck you up against this door like a goddamn animal? You *undo* me, sunshine."

"I don't want gentle. I just want you inside me."

With my hips pinning her to the door, her pussy grinding down on me, I fumbled for the condom in my wallet and then shoved my pants down far enough to tug out my cock. I sheathed it as fast as fucking possible, knowing what was waiting for me between Hannah's thighs. What was going to welcome me home.

"Can't even go a day without getting inside this pussy, can I?" I pushed into her, forcing myself to give her my inches nice and slow. No matter how wet she was, her face always contorted with that beautiful mixture of pleasure and pain when I slid inside, and I wanted to make damn sure I gave her more pleasure than anything else. "How the fuck did I last twelve goddamn years without it?"

"Don't know, but it's yours now."

Mine. Everything ceased to exist but the feeling of Hannah's pussy milking my cock, her walls already fluttering with how close she was to her release. One of her hands clutched behind my neck, holding my face to hers, greedy with her mouth on mine, while the other dug into my ass, urging me to go faster, harder, deeper. And I gave her everything I had, gripping her hips as I slammed her down on my cock over and over again, working us both toward the peak we were desperate to reach together.

When we did, when we fell into the chasm below, our names whispered groans between us, I knew there was no way I was ever going back to how things used to be. No way I could ever let Hannah walk out of my life. Not now, not after I'd had a taste of her perfection.

chapter eight

"LUKE," I MURMURED, my thighs shaking and my nerves still firing shots of sensation through me. The man made me boneless, giving me the sort of pleasure every woman had probably dreamed of at some point.

He was still inside me, holding me up as he panted into my neck. There was no space between us, no separation. And already, I wanted him again even if we were still standing up inside a janitor's closet. It didn't matter. I couldn't stop thinking about him, couldn't stop seeking him out when we were apart. I'd spent the entire evening watching him out of the corner of my eye, wishing we could be together in some way. Needing to feel his hands on me.

"Luke, you have to—"

"Shh." His lips were warm as he kissed my neck,

his hands strong as he kneaded my ass and slid out of me. "I know. Let me get you cleaned up, then we can go back to the party."

My feet hit the floor, Luke's hands supporting me, but I was still too far gone. Too high on the endorphins running through my body. Luke turned to grab something, but I clung to his shoulder. Unable to let go even as the reality that I'd have to settled over me—that this was our last night together before it was time to go home.

I had to know. "What do we do tomorrow?"

"Don't worry about that now. We'll figure it out." He gave me a quick kiss, as if that could calm the raging emotions inside of me, then wiped away the evidence of us from between my legs. Paper towel and condom tossed into the trash, he tugged my dress back down, his hands gentle, his smile soft on his lips. "We've got one more night together before reality creeps in, and I want to enjoy every second of it."

Something about those words, about the way he seemed to be ignoring the future, only reminded me that this wouldn't last. It was a fling. A weekend of fun and sex. Nothing more.

No matter how much I might now want it to be.

"Right. No jumping ahead," I whispered before running my fingers through the ends of my hair and tightening my updo. At least I could look put together on the outside. "We should get out there before people realize we're both gone."

Luke's hands worked the button on his dark jeans, the ones I'd been admiring all night, and his shirt wasn't tucked in yet. Too bad. I couldn't wait anymore, couldn't breathe in that tiny space. The pressure of not knowing, of needing to put all my trust in something so unsure, was too much. I pressed down on the handle and swung the door wide in my effort to escape.

"Wait, sunshine." Luke raced up behind me and knocked into my hip, steadying me with an arm around my waist as I came to a stop. One that wasn't because he'd called my nickname.

"Sunshine?" Barry said, his voice dripping with sarcasm. "You sob about the people who come through your emergency room and walk around with blood on your shoes, but he calls you sunshine? That's rich."

"Barry—"

"Save it." His glower sent ice flying up my spine. "I'm not taking any of your shit after this."

"Hey," Luke barked, taking a step in front of me. Protecting me, a move even Barry seemed to notice if his eyebrow raise was any indication. "Keep talking to her like that, and you're gonna see what it feels like to be on the receiving end of my fist."

"I'll talk to her any way I like. She's *my* girlfriend."

Jackass. "No, I'm not."

"Oh, really?"

Luke clenched his hands into fists, and a muscle in his jaw jumped. "Hannah says she's not, and I'm inclined to believe her."

Barry's face went red, and he stepped right up into Luke's space, staring him down hard. "You know goddamned well she's mine. She's been with me since high school, and what? Now you think you can rush in and steal her from me?"

"Just repaying the favor," Luke spat with a wicked sort of scowl. "You always did want everything I set my eyes on, didn't you?"

I inched forward, unwilling to let Luke take the brunt of the blame. "I'm not yours, Barry. I haven't been in a long time."

"Shut up, Hannah."

Luke shot forward, shoving Barry in the shoulder and almost knocking him down. "I warned you, asshole. One more word to her, and I won't stop with a little push."

"Stop this," I yelled, trying to get between the two but failing as Luke dragged me back behind him. "You two are brothers. You can't fight like this."

"Brothers. Right." Barry's words couldn't have sounded more sarcastic or harsh. "How the fuck did I end up with a brother who steals my girl?"

"I haven't been your brother in a long damn time. You made sure of that."

"So you think you can just fuck my girl for the weekend to prove you're the bigger man?" Barry caught my eye, looking downright gleeful in a malevolent sort of way when he pinned me with his glare. "What? You didn't fall for his act, did you? Did you think Luke here would want more than a fling just to piss me off?"

"I—"

Luke cut me off, still completely focused on Barry.

Only Barry. "What I want with Hannah is between her and me and has nothing to do with you."

But Barry's words hit home the way they always had, extinguishing any fire I'd stoked within me. "Stop it, Barry."

He laughed, throwing his head back as if I'd just told the best joke ever. "You did! Oh, this is perfect. What are you going to do, Hannah? Drive two hours here after a twelve-hour shift so you can cry to him about the poor kids who came through the hospital? Do you really believe anyone other than me will sit and listen to your complaining? Because, let me tell you, it's not easy. I may not have been perfect, but at least I was close enough to take care of you when you needed me to."

I shook my head, backing away from both of them. "You cheated. A lot."

"You think he's going to be the faithful one?" Barry shouted, throwing an arm toward an almost stunned looking Luke. "What…he's going to be sitting here all alone on the island as you work yourself half to death? He owns a fucking brewery, Hannah. The man sees more pussy than a gynecologist."

"Luke wouldn't do that to me—he wouldn't lie like that."

There was something about the way Barry's face contorted, about the gleam that burned in his eyes, that sent a warning up my spine.

"You think he's going to tell you everything, sweetheart? I bet he never told you about the time he caught me with another woman in our apartment.

Your knight in shining armor forget to mention he knew I was cheating on you and kept it to himself?"

Luke had become the living embodiment of anger, shooting daggers with his eyes. "You're trying to paint *me* as the bad guy when you're the one who screwed around on her? Unfuckingbelievable. You had no idea what you had when she was yours, but I'm glad you were too stupid to realize it."

Barry sneered. "My dad may have been fooled by you, but I'm not. I've always known you were nothing. Bet your mom's real fucking proud of you, too. Trash begets trash."

Luke lunged at Barry like some sort of animal. He swung his arm wide, landing a solid punch to Barry's nose before throwing another punch into Barry's gut that left him doubled over. The two grappled, slamming into the lockers more than once as they each tried to overpower the other.

Me? I stood stock-still, unable to look away, unable to stop thinking about what Barry had said. Luke—my sweet, caring friend who'd always been so kind to me—had lied. He'd known Barry betrayed me, and he'd hung me out to dry. He had allowed Barry to humiliate me for God knew how long before I'd finally confronted the asshole, and I'd let him seduce me. I'd let Luke weasel his way into my heart in a more-than-friends sort of way, unaware that I'd been betrayed by him already.

What could I expect if I pushed for a relationship outside of this weekend fling? More of the same? Was I again relegating myself to the position of the one who was lied to? Or was this really just a fling—a couple of days of hot sex to brag about later with no chance of anything more?

I didn't want to believe it, but the truth was right in front of my eyes. Luke didn't want to make plans with me, didn't want to talk about what would happen once the weekend was over in anything more than vague terms. And he'd held back a huge secret from me.

"Stop it," I yelled. "Stop fighting, both of you."

Luke stopped first, turning just enough to look my way. Big mistake. Barry took the opportunity to sucker-punch him in the jaw, though apparently, he'd forgotten how strong the facial bones were in comparison to the hand ones.

"Motherfucker," Barry yelled, shaking out his fist.

"You never could throw a solid punch." Luke rubbed his jaw, putting space between him and his brother.

"Fuck you."

"Are we done here?" I asked, arms crossed, glaring at the two of them. When neither man said anything, I took a deep breath. "Barry, you're an asshole. You treat me like shit, you treat Luke like shit, and you even treat his mom, the woman who raised you like you were her own, like shit. You've got a nice career going for you, but that's literally all you have. It's sad to me, but I can't worry about you anymore. We're through, which means I don't want you anywhere near my life."

Barry scoffed, not bothering to look at me. "Yeah, right."

"Don't doubt me on this. I've let you get away

with treating me like shit for too long. It won't be happening again. And you." I pointed at Luke. "You should have told me about Barry and the other woman."

Luke sighed, his brow pulling down. "I thought you were happy with him. I didn't want to hurt you."

Something snapped inside of me. Something hard and sharp that had been holding back a lot of anger. A lot of pain. Something that had left me weakened. It burst, and my heart filled with a fury I didn't know if I could control. "Bullshit, Luke. That's a child's excuse. What are we, twelve? Can we act like adults for five minutes?"

"No." Barry wiped the blood still falling from his nose and spat on the floor. "I'm done being an adult. You want her, brother dearest? She's yours."

It wasn't his place to give me to anyone, but I wasn't about to correct him right then. I had bigger fish to fry. "Don't show up at my door, and don't come back trying to charm me into bed with you again. Do us both a favor and lose my number, because I won't be using yours."

Barry startled, seeming shocked by my words or the fierceness of my voice. Either way, he didn't have it in him to respond. He walked past me, not even pausing as he disappeared around a corner.

He left Luke and me alone, the hall quiet except for the whisper of the music playing in the gym on the other side of the school. But I wasn't a teenager anymore; I wasn't one to make decisions I knew could be bad and hope they'd work out. No matter how many movies would claim different, no one ever tamed the bad boy of the school. And while Luke wasn't really bad, he was a threat. To me. To my heart. I'd been Barry's doormat for years. I wasn't about to be the occasional hookup for the guy who would probably lie to me, too.

"I think it's time to leave," I said, turning away from Luke and heading for the gym. Alone. A move that was both intentional and symbolic.

"Where are we going?"

"Not we, Luke." I shook my head, my steps growing faster. My mind made up. "I don't want to be around you right now."

Luke grabbed my arm, spinning me around. "Why the hell not?"

"You lied!" I pushed out of his hold. "You knew Barry was cheating, and you chose not to tell me."

"I didn't tell you because I gave my asshole brother the chance to do something right, to tell you on his own." He took a step closer, one I refused to back away from, and dropped his voice to be softer. "I swear I didn't know it wasn't the only time, Hannah."

"So, what? I'm just supposed to trust you now? I'm supposed to forget you kept this huge secret from me because you thought your fear of seeing me hurting was more important than me being hurt?"

"No, that's not—"

"Tell me something, Luke… What are we going to do on Monday when we both need to get back to work?"

"Whatever we—"

"And what about on Thursday, when I have to work a double and will probably be a pile of ragged emotions at the end of it? What will we do?"

"Hannah, I'm not—"

"I've been with a man for twelve years who could barely be there for me, and he lived with me for part of that time. How are you going to support me when you're two hours away?"

Growling, he clung to my arms, his hold hard, his voice dripping with something that sounded an awful lot like anger. "Would you let me talk? What, in our twelve-year history, has given you the impression I wouldn't support you? In every-fucking-thing. Two hours or two minutes away, I'll be there for you, Hannah. You *know* that."

"A twelve-year history with a giant, gaping wound because you couldn't tell me the truth. Even though he treated you and your mom like second-class citizens, you chose Barry over me when the chips were down."

"I did *not* choose Barry over you. I would never. I've wanted you for twelve long years, and that hasn't changed. If I could go back, I never would've told Barry about my feelings for you. I should've known he'd swoop in before I even had a chance. Seeing you together all these years about killed me. You think I chose him over you? You were *always* my choice, Hannah. Even when you weren't mine."

"I'm still not yours, Luke." I stepped back. Walking away even though every inch between us caused fractures in my heart. Knowing it was time to go home despite how much it hurt to do so. "Look, this just isn't going to work. I can't keep making the same mistakes."

"What we had these past two days was not a mistake."

"I don't know if two days can make up for everything, Luke. I really don't. Not anymore."

Luke reached for me, looking almost lost as his hand brushed against my cheek. "Sunshine, don't leave like this. Tell me what I need to do. How can I make this right?"

Not a single answer popped into my head. There was simply nothing—no bright eyes, no tattooed arms, no Luke. My mind had already shut him out, a fact that made me want to curl up in a ball right there and cry. Instead, I pulled away from his touch. "I don't know if you can. Finding out you knew—you were there, you saw her, and you said nothing—it hurts. It's…devastating." I shook my head, the burn of tears building in my eyes sending me into a panic. I would not cry in front of him. I would not. "I'm leaving, and I need you to let me do that."

"Fine. If that's what you need to do, leave." His jaw clenched, and he finally stopped reaching for me, something that made the hurt even worse. "But I'm going to come after you, Hannah. I'm going to fight for you. For *us*. I'm not going to let you slip through my fingers this time."

I nodded, waiting for…something. It took me a few seconds to realize he was serious. He was letting me go. Barry would have cornered me, would have refused to let me take a step until I bent to his will.

Luke…wasn't Barry. The pain on Luke's face was obvious, his struggle to let me go plain, but he didn't fight me. He didn't try to overwhelm me. He let me make my own decisions, which was both amazing and saddening. This was all on me, and I was going to have to live with the consequences if I was wrong.

But what if I was right?

I spun and hurried to the gym so I could grab my bag, confusion muddling my thoughts. All but one—I was done here. Temperance Falls, as much as I loved it, would never be home again. I needed to face that. To move forward with the life I'd chosen. And to find someone willing to move forward with me.

"Where have you been?" Jessica asked when I reached the table. She was sitting on Aaron's lap, looking happy and more than a little tipsy. "We've been looking for you."

"I'm not feeling well." I was an asshole, but I could hate myself for lying later. "I'm taking off."

"Want me to pick up some ginger ale on the way back home?"

"No, I won't be there. I'm going back to the city."

Her smile fell, and she suddenly looked a little more sober. "What about Luke?"

And wasn't that the question of the night? What about him? I shrugged, trying to play like my heart wasn't breaking. "Luke's a big boy. He'll be okay."

"Hannah," Jessica said, but I didn't let her finish. I grabbed her and Aaron in a hug instead.

"Thank you for your hospitality. I'm going to pack up my stuff and get out of your hair."

And with that, I walked out of the high school where everything had started so long ago. It was time to be done with childish things.

———

The drive home seemed endless, taking so much longer since I had to keep pulling over to give myself time to stop crying. Still, I made it back to my little apartment with its boring tan rug and walls, its tiny kitchen only meant for one person. The place was silent and cold, and I hated it. There was no Luke there. I hated it, but it was where my life resided. Too exhausted to do anything else, I turned off the lights and headed to my bedroom, ready to put the weekend behind me. Ready to sleep away the painful rock that had wedged itself in my chest and refused to let me breathe.

On Sunday, I went to work. I wasn't scheduled and probably needed the time off to put my head back on straight, but when the charge nurse called that she needed help, I jumped. The beigeness of my place had started to suffocate me. Fuck sitting home alone and wallowing—work would keep my mind off of things.

Or so I thought.

Instead, I spent eight hours on my feet, my heart aching, and my mind constantly drifting to Luke. What was he doing? Did he miss me at all? Was he glad I'd left, or had I hurt him with my disappearing act? What had I been thinking? Luke wasn't Barry—he wasn't the type of guy who would cheat on his girl. At least, I didn't think so. There had to be a good reason for why he hadn't told me about Barry and the other woman. It wasn't his way to be dishonest. Or was that my crush overriding what my brain was trying to tell me? Was this like when Barry was cheating and I'd started to see the signs of it but chose to ignore them? If I called Luke and told him I missed him, would I regret it later when something went wrong?

It was all too much, too overwhelming. I needed a break from my own mind.

"Just keep nursing. Just keep nursing—"

"You okay, Hannah?" The admin behind the front desk gave me a funny look, her eyes seeming to take in every detail. Wonderful. I'd ripped a hole in my life the likes of which I wasn't sure I could fix, and now my coworkers were going to think I had lost my mind.

I dropped the pen I'd been holding, the one that hadn't made a single note on the chart I'd laid out probably fifteen minutes ago. No wonder I was being questioned. "I'm fine, just tired. I chant to myself to keep going when I'm tired."

"Like that fish from the movie."

Okay, then. "Yeah, exactly. Like that."

She smiled and turned back around. "Whatever works to get you through the day. You do look tired."

Which meant I looked like shit. Of course. "I'm fine. Really."

"It's not my business," she said, sneaking a peek

over her shoulder at me. "But you look like your heart's been ripped out and stomped on."

My breath caught, and I wasn't sure what to say. Not at first. Not until I stopped thinking and just let the words come. "He didn't mean to."

"That's good. That means things can get put back together." She rose to her feet, a stack of old charts in her arms. "I need to get these back down to storage. You take it easy on yourself."

Her words echoed in my head for the rest of the day. *Things can get put back together.* I wasn't sure if I believed them, but they wouldn't let me go. Wouldn't let me refuse them and go back into a neat little box where I could ignore the possibility.

Things can get put back together… but only if we both wanted to do the work. He'd let me make the choice to walk away, which meant I was probably going to have to be the first one to reach out if I wanted to fix things. I wasn't sure if I was ready for that just yet.

After my shift ended, I trudged home and crawled into the shower. I needed to wash the day off me. To wash the confusion down the drain. It didn't seem to work. All I could think about as I stared at my bathroom vanity was Luke bending me over the counter back at Aaron and Jessica's place. How he'd whispered filthy things to me. How he'd held me so tight, as if he hadn't wanted to let me go. I'd never felt as safe as I had in his arms, never felt as loved as I did when he wrapped me up in his body and held on. How could I walk away from that?

How could he let me?

chapter nine

LUKE

AFTER SO LONG without Hannah in my bed, a single day should've been a cakewalk. I should've been able to give her the space she clearly needed. Should've been able to go about my day as usual like all the days prior to this weekend, not thinking about her but in the barest sense I'd allowed myself.

But things were different now.

All those years had gone by because I hadn't known the taste of her lips or the feel of her tight little body under mine. I hadn't known the sweetness of her whispering my name as she came around me. Hadn't known the sound of her hushed laughter at three in the morning as I discovered all her ticklish spots.

And I wanted it *back*. More than anything, I wanted her. I needed to reassure her that she was my number one priority now, and I'd never keep anything from her again. The real kicker about this whole situation was that my asshole brother was still keeping us apart, this time with just his words. And it pissed me off.

Now, she was two hours away from me, and I had no fucking idea how long I should wait before going after her and fighting for us, just like I told her I would. I'd wanted to give her an hour and then follow her over the bridge and into the city. Wanted to show up at her door at midnight and tell her all the reasons we were perfect together, all the reasons she shouldn't turn her back on us. But I'd promised I'd let her go. I just didn't know how long was long enough. It'd been twenty hours since I'd last seen her, and already it felt like my heart was eating itself.

"Whoa, dude," AJ said, taking away a glass I was drying. "You remember how much time we spent painstakingly picking and choosing the perfect mugs to carry?"

"What?" I asked, having no idea what he was talking about.

"*These*." He waved a hand at the line of mugs I'd placed on the counter. "These glorious specimens of beer-toting goodness do *not* deserve your anger, asshole. Slamming them down on the bartop like they're fucking rubber balls, Jesus Christ." He shook his head. "Take it out on something a little less breakable, huh?"

"Shit, sorry." I scrubbed a hand down my face and sagged against the bar, tossing the drying towel over my shoulder. It wasn't quite four in the afternoon, which meant I had little time to get my shit together before our doors opened for the night. Not enough time.

"You gonna tell me what's got your panties in a twist? You've been cranky as hell all day." AJ raised an eyebrow. "With your texts over the weekend, I assumed you'd met up with a hottie and were passing the storm with some good old-fashioned fucking. And now you're all mopey and shit. Since when does Luke Markos get mopey?"

"Since I *did* meet up with a hottie, and that hottie was Hannah."

AJ whipped his head around to stare at me, mouth agape. "Hannah? As in, *the* Hannah? Your asshole of a stepbrother's girlfriend, Hannah?"

"*Ex*-girlfriend. And, yes, idiot. How many fucking Hannahs have I talked about?"

"Just the one, but I had to be sure."

"Yeah, well. Now you are."

He whistled low. "So you got with Hannah. You said ex-girlfriend, so Barry's not the problem—"

"Barry's *always* the problem."

"What'd the fucknut do this time?"

Blowing out a deep sigh, I tossed the towel onto the bartop and crossed my arms over my chest. "He caught us, and everything went to shit after that."

"Caught you? Doing what?"

I raised an eyebrow. "What do you think?"

"No shit? Where?"

"Janitor's closet at the high school."

He gave an appreciative nod. "*Nice.*"

"Not the time, man."

"Right, sorry."

"He told her about when I found him with that other woman. Made it out like I'd purposely kept something from her."

"God, I hate that fucker. Always have."

"I'm finally starting to understand why."

"It's about damn time."

"Yeah, well." I shook my head, running a hand through my hair in frustration. "He's still working his games. Keeping Hannah and me apart, even without him in the picture anymore."

"How's that? Why aren't you at her place right now?"

"He told her all that shit, and then she said she didn't know if she could trust me. Said she wanted to leave. Without me."

"So you let her leave. Good call, but that was last night. What're you still doing here?"

"What do you mean, what am I still doing here? Did you listen to the story?"

"Did *you*?"

I glanced at the clock on the wall, hoping, miraculously, it'd somehow fast-forwarded hours. Nope. "It hasn't even been twenty-four hours yet."

"Who gives a fuck?"

"*I* do. I don't want to mess this up before I've even gotten her."

"Dude." AJ sighed, shaking his head and looking at me like I was a toddler. "I don't know why I have to dole out the relationship advice, but here we are." He gripped me by the shoulders and shook me a little. "You're an idiot. Go."

"Go where?"

"Her house. Jesus Christ, Luke, did you literally fuck your brains out this weekend?" He smacked me upside the head, then danced away before I could retaliate. "Get in your car, drive over the bridge, find her place, and knock on her door. It's not rocket science, man."

"What if I haven't given her enough time?"

He shot his brows up. "Ever think she might be as miserable as you?"

I sure as hell hoped not. "But Hops—"

"Isn't hoppin' yet, and when it is, we'll handle it. Been picking up for your slack-ass all weekend, anyway. What's another day?" And with that, he shoved me toward the back, tossing my keys at me before pushing me outside and slamming the door in my face. "You can thank me later," he shouted through the closed door.

I stared down at my keys, then glanced at my watch—again. But who cared what time it was? The only time I knew was *too fucking long away from Hannah*. I didn't know if there was some rule I was supposed to follow, if I should've called first or warned her I was coming. But the beginning of our…whatever this was…hadn't been conventional. Why should I start now?

Without another thought, I hopped in my Jeep and took off toward the bridge and then to her place, thankful I had her address stored in my phone.

Hitting rush hour once on the mainland made the trip longer than it should've been, which only added to my frustration.

After too fucking long, I pulled up in front of her apartment, luckily finding a spot close, even on the busy street. The five-story brick building looked like it'd seen better days, but I'd passed the hospital only a couple blocks down, so I assumed that was why she'd picked it. I headed inside, scowling over the fact that there wasn't any security, and took the stairs two at a time to get to her floor.

I didn't stop before I knocked on her door. Didn't take a minute to figure out what the fuck I was going to say, or how I was going to approach this. I just knew I was there, within a few feet of her, and I couldn't wait a second more to see her face.

She answered without questioning who was there, just opened the door, her head down as she dug through her wallet. Wet hair framed her makeup-free face, and she wore nothing but a short robe, the front dipping down into a V. Jesus fucking Christ.

Finally, she glanced up at me as she extended a handful of cash, a polite and bland smile on her face. At least until her eyes connected with mine—until she realized who was on the other side of her door. The smile dropped, the cash and her wallet fell to the floor, and she stared, slack-jawed.

"Luke—"

"You always answer your door in a robe without checking to see who's on the other side?"

"I ordered a pizza."

Scowling at her probably wasn't the best way to start this conversation, but nobody else needed to see her like this, especially considering she was probably completely bare underneath. "You're wearing a *robe*, Hannah."

"I..." She straightened, tightening said robe around her. "What are you doing here?"

I reached for her, ran my finger down her cheek. "I came for you. I told you I'd fight for us, didn't I?"

A throat cleared to my right. "Uh...sorry to interrupt."

I glanced over my shoulder to see a young guy in a red baseball hat, holding a pizza warmer.

"I have a Hawaiian pizza for"—the red-faced delivery guy glanced at the receipt—"Hannah Fedele?"

"That's me." Hannah bent down to grab her money, the front of her robe gaping open. If I'd been behind her, I had no doubt I'd have gotten a glimpse of her pussy, too.

As fast as I could, I slid in front of her, blocking the pimply faced teenager's view and shooting him a glare. "You want a tip?" I snapped. "Keep your eyes up here."

"Jesus, Luke. Give the guy a break." She passed the delivery guy a handful of cash. "Sorry. He's territorial, apparently."

"N-no problem, thanks." He stuffed the money into his pocket and rushed toward the stairwell.

I turned back to Hannah, gripping her by the elbow and leaning in until my mouth was against her ear. "Your tits were on full view when you bent over, so how about next time you don't answer the door in your robe unless you know it's me."

A shiver racked her body before she straightened her spine and pulled away, holding the door open for me. "Next time, huh? Pretty presumptuous considering how we left things yesterday."

I stepped inside, locking her door behind me and following her into her small galley kitchen. "Not presumptuous...*hopeful*. I don't take on fights unless I think I can win, and I'm fighting for this."

She pulled down two plates from the cabinet by the sink, then grabbed a couple cans of pop from the fridge, hip checking it to close the door. Acting like my being in her space was an everyday occurrence. She wanted to play normal? I could do that.

"Maybe I'm tired of fighting," she said. "Maybe I just want things to be easy for once."

I followed her lead, placing a couple slices of pizza on the plates and following her into the living room. It was...not at all what I expected. No color, no *life*. Not at all Hannah.

Settling next to her on the couch, I handed her a plate. "Then how about you sit there and look pretty, and I'll do all the fighting?"

She shot me an unamused smile. "Be serious."

"I *am* being serious. If I have to spend hours, days, weeks, fighting for this, then I will." I took a bite of the pizza. It was no supreme, but this was her favorite and always had been, so I sucked it up. "Do you know why?"

She shrugged and took a sip of her pop. "Because you love beating Barry at everything?"

Was that really what she thought this was? Time to clear that up real quick. "Because I love *you*. And because you deserve someone who thinks you're important enough to be willing to do anything to keep you." I polished off my first piece and started in on the second.

Rolling her eyes, she set her slice of pizza on her plate. If I weren't paying such close attention, I would've missed how her hand shook. "So now you think you love me?"

"I don't think, I know." I reached out, swiping my thumb over the corner of her mouth where she had a bit of pizza sauce. "And if you believe you're going to find someone who'll love you harder than I will, you're wrong. I've loved you for more than a decade, sunshine. I'm not stopping anytime soon."

She bit her lip, glancing down before meeting my eyes. "If you loved me, then why did you lie to me? Why did you let Barry get away with what he did?"

I blew out a breath, hating that my asshole of a stepbrother was still fucking this up. "I didn't let him get away with it. I caught him and told him he'd tell you or I would. I sometimes wish it *had* come from me, but I gave him the chance to make amends."

"He never told me he was cheating, Luke. I found him with another woman in our bed."

"What? No, he called me and told me he'd come clean, that you guys were going to counseling—even gave me the fucking counselor's name. He said you were upset but wanted to try to make it work…"

She'd started shaking her head before I'd even finished. "Never happened. I found them, and two days later, I moved in to this place. There was no counseling." She laughed. "Though, can you imagine Barry in a counseling session? I have no idea how you believed that one."

I ground my teeth together. Once again, I'd let my loyalty to him cloud my judgment.

Never again.

"I should've known. I…" I blew out a breath. "I just wanted you to be happy. Even if it wasn't with me. After all those years of his bullshit and lies, I should've been able to see through him, but he'd made it sound like you were happy…with him. And you never mentioned anything whenever we talked…" I placed my plate on the coffee table, then scrubbed a hand down my face. "Maybe if I *had* seen through him, you and I would be somewhere else now."

"Like where?" she asked, her voice soft. She leaned toward me, her plate discarded on the table.

"Where?" I reached out, brushing her damp hair behind her ear, then trailed my finger across her jaw and down her neck, smiling as goose bumps erupted on her skin. "Name it. Temperance Falls, here, my bedroom, fucking Japan—as long as we were together, it wouldn't matter where."

She leaned into the hand I'd wrapped around her neck, my thumb brushing against her pulse point. "How would we make it work? Right here and now…how would we be a couple when you live on the island and I'm here?"

I straightened, darting my eyes between hers, not even attempting to push down the hope climbing up my throat. "However we needed to. Temperance Falls isn't that far away. I'd drive here. You can drive there. Weekends, vacations… And in between, there's always phone sex." I shot her a smirk.

She laughed and ducked her face. "You're not exactly the type of guy I see being satisfied with phone sex."

I narrowed my eyes, trying to get a read on her. Trying to figure out what she was really asking. "This isn't just any phone sex we're talking about—it's phone sex with *you*." With a finger under her chin, I turned her head so she looked at me. "Is this about what Barry said?"

She shrugged. "I could never make him happy, and knowing I could disappoint you…that I might not be enough…"

"Sunshine…" Even though we were only six inches apart, it was too much. I gripped her by the hips and tugged her right into my lap, settling her knees on either side of my hips. Willing my cock to settle the fuck down because now was not the time to get hard. Or harder, as it were. I cupped her face, pulling her down so I could feel her breath against my mouth. "You made me happy when we weren't together. If you were *mine*? I'd be the happiest man on the whole fucking planet."

She closed the last couple inches, brushing her

lips against mine. "Even if you don't get to see me every day?"

Groaning, I covered her mouth with mine, unable to stop when she was so close. Unable to stop from tasting her, from pressing against the small of her back and grinding her down on me. To hell with acting like just being around her didn't get me hard as steel. Let her feel what she did to me.

I pulled away, pressing a kiss to the corner of her mouth. "Even then." I trailed my hands up and down her back as she melted into me. "If you were mine, you'd know that means I'd be yours, too. Just yours."

Hannah sighed into my mouth, her hands fisting the front of my T-shirt as she slid her tongue against mine. Jesus, had it really only been a day since I'd last tasted her? Since I'd last swallowed her breathy moans, since she'd ground herself down on my cock? How the hell was I going to last when we were apart?

Didn't matter *how*, just that I would. I'd deal with it, doing whatever it took to make this work between us. Hannah was worth every bit of sacrifice I could possibly make. And I'd make them all for her.

"Luke?" She panted, tipping her head to the side when I moved my lips down her neck. "Will you stay with me tonight?"

And every night for as long as she'd have me. With her ass gripped in my hands, I stood from the couch and walked down the short hall, finding her bedroom on the second try, my attention distracted as she nipped at my neck all the while grinding down on my cock. "Shit, sunshine." I kneaded her ass, pushing her against me. "I didn't bring a change of clothes, so that means a lot of naked time."

"Oh, damn." She pushed away from me, and I reluctantly let her down until she stood in front of me. And then she untied her robe and let it pool at her feet. I knew it—completely fucking bare. "Better be careful. It gets chilly in here at night."

"I can see that," I said, my voice low and gruff. "Or, are these for me?" I gripped her around the waist and leaned down, taking one pert nipple between my lips.

Her hands flew to my hair, holding me to her as she moaned deep in her throat. I smiled around her breast before switching sides, sucking her deep and making her arch into me. Her tits were small and perky and so fucking responsive.

"Someday, we're going to see if I can make you come with just my mouth on your tits."

"Not today?"

"No, not today," I said as I guided her toward her bed and didn't stop until she was lying in the middle, her legs spread the tiniest bit. Goddamn, she was a fucking goddess, and I hadn't yet had a chance to really *look* at her. This weekend had been about rushed, secret encounters. But, tonight? Tonight, I was going to savor.

She made a move to cover her breasts, no doubt uncomfortable as I stood there and stared.

"You remember what I said the first time in the boathouse?" I waited for her nod before continuing. "Good, then you know I want to look at every inch of you."

"But you're still dressed."

"You want me naked, sunshine? You just had to ask."

"Please. I want to see you."

I didn't take my time stripping down, instead ridding myself of my clothes as quickly as fucking possible. I grabbed my wallet and dug out the backup condom, tossing it on the pillow next to her head. "Should've brought a box with me."

She giggled, her tits bouncing slightly with the movement. "I don't think we can go through a whole box tonight."

"No?" I asked, picking up her leg and pressing a kiss on her ankle. Letting my tongue stroke the sensitive skin. I moved slowly up her leg, brushing my mouth over every inch of her. "I think we might need two."

Her laughter cut off on a moan when I licked the crease between her leg and her pussy. "Luke…"

"Hmm?" I asked as I started the torture on the other leg, working my way up to where she was already swollen and wet for me.

"I want you inside me."

"'Fraid I can't do that yet, sunshine."

"Why?" she asked, shifting under my wandering mouth. "I'm…I'm wet enough."

Just to torture us both, I ran a finger through her slit, spreading her wetness. "That you are. Dripping just for my cock, isn't that right?"

"*Yes.*"

"Do you know why I can't give it to you yet?" I asked, then licked across the top of her mound.

She groaned, slipping her fingers into my hair and trying to push me down to where she wanted me. Seemed forty-eight hours of me worshiping her pussy with my tongue was enough to get her past her hesitance in that area.

"No answer?" I teased, dragging my bottom lip across her lower stomach as she panted, her head tossing back and forth on the pillow. "Because I'm going to worship this beautiful body. I'm going to spend as long as it takes until you realize you"—I nipped at the slight flare of her hip—"are the only one I want." I moved up, licking the underside of each breast. "That I love each bit of you, want your scent all over me." I moved down her body again until I hovered over her pussy, then I leaned in and swiped my tongue straight through her slit, letting it flick hard against her clit.

She gasped and bucked up against my mouth, using her grip on my hair to tug me closer. "There, Luke. Please, there."

"You want me to lick your pussy? Suck this sweet little clit into my mouth?"

"God, yes."

I licked her once more, then pulled back, using my fingers instead. "I will, but first I need to tell you something."

"*Now?*"

"Yes, now. And I need you to believe me."

"Anything, Luke, just please—" She moaned as I pinched her clit between my fingers.

"Listen. Are you listening?"

"Yes, yes…"

"A million women could come prancing through the brewery, buck-ass naked, and not a single one would turn my head." I showed her mercy, stilling her rolling hips with my hands, my thumbs pointed toward her pussy to spread her wide open for me. Her clit was swollen and peeking out from under the hood, just begging for my mouth. "Not when I get to call you mine."

"Oh God, I'll be yours, Luke. Only yours."

Christ, hearing that, I couldn't wait another minute. I sucked her clit between my lips, sliding two fingers into her pussy and groaning at how wet she was. Gone was the shy girl who didn't even want me to give her a lick. In her place was a woman who was too desperate to come to care what she did. With her hands clutched in my hair, she ground her pussy against my tongue, rolling her hips in the perfect rhythm to send her hurtling toward her climax.

"Shit, I'm gonna come. Luke, I'm—"

Not daring to stop what I was doing, I groaned against her, licking her as she screamed her release, no longer needing to stifle the sound.

When her tremors finally ceased and her hips stopped rolling, she tightened her fingers in my hair. "Now?" she asked, trying to slow her breathing.

I reached for the condom, sheathing myself before settling between her spread thighs and sliding into her, nice and slow. "Now," I said, kissing up her neck as I lifted her thigh up and over my hip, sliding even deeper into her.

I caught her moan in my mouth, kissing her as I pumped into her body—the body that fit so perfectly against mine it was like she was made for me. After twelve years, there was no way in hell I was letting her go.

"Now," I said again as I rocked us toward our release. "Always."

BEING WITHOUT HANNAH while we'd lived it two different places had been exactly as hard as we'd thought it would be. It'd meant late nights and early mornings, hundreds upon hundreds of miles put on my Jeep as we'd worked around Hannah's hellish schedule, and an expert understanding of Skype.

Jesus, the Skype calls. Even better than phone sex? *Video* sex.

There'd been the reassurances, too. After she'd spent so long with an asshole like Barry, I made it my mission to show her exactly what it was like to be with someone who loved her more than himself. Someone who would drop what he was doing and drive two hours after she'd had someone code in the ER and needed a warm body to snuggle with to help wash away the memories. Someone who would order her Hawaiian pizza and have it paid for and delivered when she was too exhausted from a double to even think straight. Someone who made sure her gas tank was always full and her favorite coffee was always stocked. It'd turned out washing away her fears and apprehensions had been easy, considering I put her first in everything and Barry never had.

As for him, he'd come slinking back to Hannah only a couple weeks after she'd told him never to come by again—just like I'd known he would. Fortunately, it'd happened on a night I'd been staying there. Answering the door in just my boxer briefs and telling him Hannah was passed out on the bed and too hoarse from screaming to hold a conversation was probably a dick move, but it got the point across. He never bothered her again.

And Barry's and my relationship? It was exactly as dead as he'd left it ten years ago. I no longer had the compulsion or the desire to breathe life into it just to keep it afloat. So I let it go.

As much as I hated him for what he'd done to Hannah, I also had to admit he played a role in where Hannah and I found ourselves now. Which was, finally, back in Temperance Falls. Together.

Yesterday, I'd borrowed a truck from a friend and went and got my girlfriend. Hannah hadn't wanted to keep much of her stuff, selling off most of her furnishings one by one when she'd gotten the job offer at Temperance Falls Hospital. She'd said her apartment had never felt like hers, anyway. So we'd packed up what she'd wanted to and driven home…where she belonged.

It hadn't even been twenty-four hours yet, and

already I was antsy as hell because she wasn't by my side. We'd separated that morning, me going to the brewery and Hannah saying she'd come by and see me before too long.

Too long had turned into hours, which had turned me into an asshole. Rain battered the roof of Pops' Hops, making my cock tighten in my jeans. Ever since the boathouse, when I'd tasted her for the first time with the sound of the storm going on outside, the rain always made me horny as fuck. Hannah shared my sentiment, sometimes waking me up in the middle of the night if a thunderstorm rolled in, stroking my cock until it was hard as a rock and then hopping on to take what she needed.

And yet she wasn't here.

"Don't tell me I have to give you another lecture about those mugs," AJ said, brow raised as he looked at the glass I was drying vigorously.

"Fuck off."

With a laugh, he shook his head, filling a glass with our specialty monthly brew for one of our regulars currently perched at the other end of the bar. "Why don't you do everyone a favor and go check on the tanks? You're going to scare off our customers with your face."

I grumbled the whole way, but I did as he suggested because the bastard was right. I couldn't help it—now that Hannah was mine, really and truly, and she was *here*, I wanted her next to me whenever fucking possible. She didn't start at the hospital for three more days, and I wanted to soak up as much of that time as I could.

Fifteen minutes later, I'd checked the tanks,

making sure all the temperatures were correct, before heading back to the front, ready to pull my hair out from all the waiting.

But there, sitting at the bar and leaning toward AJ was my girl…my sunshine. Damp strands of hair stuck to her face, her bright red Pops' Hops T-shirt spattered with rain droplets. No matter how many times I saw her, she never failed to make me stop dead in my tracks. Especially when she smiled.

I narrowed my eyes when I realized she was smiling at something AJ was saying, and with the way my jackass best friend was leaning over the counter, he was flirting and flirting hard.

Fuck and no.

"—just a year is all," AJ said as I walked toward Hannah on the other side of the bar. "Before a severe labrum tear."

"Ouch, that's a rough injury," she said. "That must've been awful, getting a chance like that and having it taken away."

I came up behind Hannah, bracing my hands on the bartop on either side of her. "Are you seriously using your 'poor me, I lost my career in the majors' bullshit on *my* girlfriend?"

Hannah leaned back against my chest, tilting her face up to look at me, and this time the smile was all for me.

AJ rested his elbow on the bartop and glanced at me, sly grin on his bastard face. "That's my best story, and you know it. Don't you have something else to do? Hannah and I were just getting reacquainted."

"I can reacquaint your ass with my boot, if you'd like."

The steel in my tone only made him laugh harder, but he knocked twice on the bartop and turned to go. "I'll see you around, Hannah."

Before she could even utter a hello, I spun her around on the seat and pulled her straight into my arms. Ducking down, I nuzzled her neck, breathing in her scent, her hair still damp from the rain. "Where've you been?"

"I'm guessing you missed me," she said, running her fingers through my hair.

Instead of answering her, I pulled back and nipped at her bottom lip.

She smiled, her hands cupping my face. "I was at your mom's. We were trying to change out her planters for the season, but the rain stopped us. She sent me home with some cookies, though. Told me to tell you not to eat them all."

Her words washed over me, soothing a place inside that had been restless since she'd left this morning. I didn't know where to start—the fact that she'd been at my mom's and how happy I was that their decade-long separation hadn't fractured their relationship, that they'd clicked again, just as they had when we'd been in high school. Or at the fact that she was already calling our place home. She'd spent a single night in our bed, in the space that was now hers, too, and already she was comfortable enough to claim it.

And I wanted us there immediately.

She brushed a finger over my brow. "What's that face for?"

"That face is because it's raining and you aren't riding my cock."

"Hmm." She leaned in, brushing her hand across the front of my jeans as she lowered her voice. "Does the brewery have a janitor's closet we can hide away in? For old time's sake?"

Oh Jesus. An internal war went on, part of me wanting to drag her back to the office, not caring who heard her scream my name, while the other part wanted her at home, in bed. Legs spread, tits on full display, riding my tongue for hours. I reached down and cupped her ass, tugging her closer. "It has an office, but I want you spread out on *our* bed."

She smiled up at me, making no move to remove her hand from between us. "Think AJ will mind if I steal you away?"

"He can deal with it." I lifted my head, calling over to him. "Hey, AJ!"

He didn't even turn around, just waved me off, telling me to get the hell out without saying a word, all the while in conversation with a customer. Then he flipped me the bird. Man, I loved my best friend. Even when he hit on my girl.

"He says he'd be glad to watch the place for a while."

Hannah laughed, pressing her forehead against my chest, then looked up at me, her lip caught between her teeth. Happiness shining in her eyes.

I reached up, brushing my thumb over her bottom lip. Fantasizing about all the things I was going to do to that mouth once we got back to our place. "You ready to go home?"

"Absolutely."

"Good, because I want to make the most of these next three days before you have to start at the hospital. And by make the most of them, I mean I want you naked as much as fucking possible and riding my cock. Or my face. I'm not picky."

"Such a charmer." With her fingers tucked into the waistband of my jeans, she walked backward toward the door, tugging me with her. "C'mon, my love. Let's go listen to the rain."

Trouble is brewing in
TEMPERANCE FALLS

The last thing a newly hired dean should be doing is one of his students...

Dirty flirting with the unbelievably hot barista at Bundt & Grind café is not how Elliott Goodridge should be spending his time. Temperance Falls College hired him to counteract a scandal—not burn through his paychecks on overpriced coffee with a side of impure thoughts.

For the amount of time college student Samantha Monroe spends fantasizing about the new guy in town, she should know more than just his name. But despite putting out all kinds of signs that she's down for, well, putting out, Elliott hasn't made a move. Yet.

By the time the truth is revealed, it's too late to stop the charge between them. Sparks fly, but so do rumors. For Elliott, a day without his hands on Sam is too long—and two orgasm-free weeks until graduation is flat-out impossible.

about the author

London Hale is the combined pen name of writing besties Ellis Leigh and Brighton Walsh. Between them, they've published more than thirty books in the contemporary romance, paranormal romance, and romantic suspense genres. Ellis is a *USA Today* bestselling author who loves coffee, thinks green Skittles are the best, and prefers to stay in every weekend. Brighton is multi-published with Berkley, St. Martin's Press, and Carina Press. She hates coffee, thinks green Skittles are the work of the devil, and has never heard of a party she didn't want to attend. Don't ask how they became such good friends or work so well together—they still haven't figured it out themselves.

www.londonhale.com